"Why are you so stubborn, Matt? Why are you so determined to get me off this case?" Annie demanded.

"You're a detective, and you need something that obvious spelled out for you," he asked, then pivoted on his heel and headed for the door.

Annie made a face at his back, then jumped up to follow him, grabbing her purse on the way.

She realized she'd misread him—or he'd changed his mind—when he suddenly closed the door and wheeled around just in time for her to crash into him and drop her purse.

His arms went around her, strong and steadying. He stared at her for several long, charged seconds. "Okay," he said roughly. "I will spell it out for you. First, I don't believe there's any real threat behind those letters. Whoever wrote them is too chicken to actually do anything. Second, if by some wild chance there is a threat, I don't want you in the line of fire. I'm not in the habit of asking anybody to fight my battles, least of all a delicate, lovely woman. And third—" He stopped, realizing Annie was in his arms, gazing up at him with an expression of shock and unmistakable desire. "Third," he said, telling himself to push her away before he did anything he'd regret, "I don't . . ." He found his lips moving over hers, his willpower and scruples dissolving instantly, as if he were being drugged by the sweet, hot taste of her. . . .

WHAT ARE *LOVESWEPT* ROMANCES?

They are stories of true romance and touching emotion. We believe those two very important ingredients are constants in our highly sensual and very believable stories in the *LOVESWEPT* line. Our goal is to give you, the reader, stories of consistently high quality that may sometimes make you laugh, sometimes make you cry, but are always fresh and creative and contain many delightful surprises within their pages.

Most romance fans read an enormous number of books. Those they truly love, they keep. Others may be traded with friends and soon forgotten. We hope that each *LOVESWEPT* romance will be a treasure—a "keeper." We will always try to publish

LOVE STORIES YOU'LL NEVER FORGET
BY AUTHORS YOU'LL ALWAYS REMEMBER

The Editors

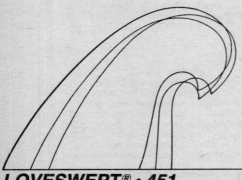

LOVESWEPT® • 451

Gail Douglas
Banned in Boston

BANTAM BOOKS
NEW YORK • TORONTO • LONDON • SYDNEY • AUCKLAND

BANNED IN BOSTON
A Bantam Book / February 1991

*LOVESWEPT® and the wave device are registered
trademarks of Bantam Books, a division of
Bantam Doubleday Dell Publishing Group, Inc.
Registered in U.S. Patent
and Trademark Office and elsewhere.*

*If you would be interested in receiving protective vinyl
covers for your Loveswept books, please write to this
address for information:*

*Loveswept
Bantam Books
P. O. Box 985
Hicksville, NY 11802*

ISBN 0-553-44096-9

Published simultaneously in the United States and Canada

*Bantam Books are published by Bantam Books, a division
of Bantam Doubleday Dell Publishing Group, Inc. Its trademark, consisting of the words "Bantam Books" and the
portrayal of a rooster, is Registered in U.S. Patent and
Trademark Office and in other countries. Marca Regis-
trada. Bantam Books, 666 Fifth Avenue, New York, New
York 10103.*

DEDICATION

To all the chili-and-beer ladies it's been my
pleasure to know.

One

Matt Harper sat behind his massive mahogany desk debating whether to laugh, swear, or raise the roof.

He decided to play it cool. The brunette with her head intriguingly tilted to one side and a grin tugging at the corners of her nicely shaped lips couldn't be serious.

She was standing beside his mother just inside his office, both women staying near the closed door like a pair of you-go-first rabbits venturing into a bear's cave on a dare. Matt was sure they were up to some prank.

Fully intending to make his visitor feel uncomfortable, Matt did a languid inventory of her. He approved of what he saw, from the tips of the young lady's black leather pumps to her shoulder-length fall of shining sable hair. She had great legs and a trim yet curvy little figure, attractively packaged in a slim black skirt, ivory silk shell, and khaki shirt-styled jacket with folded-back sleeves. Casual elegance, he mused. Very nice.

As he studied her fine-boned features a bit more carefully than he'd meant to, Matt started experiencing unexpected responses. And he had to remind himself that this woman wasn't his type. He liked his women exotic, blatantly sexy, ultrasophisticated.

Then he made the mistake of looking into a pair of huge, luminous, dark brown eyes that sparkled with curiosity and humor while hinting at a secret sensuality, and all his nerve endings leapt to attention. In the next instant, he realized that she was giving him a distinctly unsettling once-over. He blinked. How had she turned the tables so neatly? All of a sudden he was uncomfortable! "We sent for Sam Spade," he said with a growl. "How did we end up with Nancy Drew?"

"Matthew!" his mother said, her nervous-bunny act ending abruptly as she strode over to him and slapped a business card onto his desk. "Miss Brentwood took the trouble to arrive at my office at nine sharp to keep Charlie Dunhill's appointment because he couldn't make it. The least you can do is give her a decent hearing."

Picking up the card but not bothering to look at it, Matt got to his feet and walked purposefully around his desk toward the woman who'd just presented herself as a last-minute stand-in for the burly chief of Dunhill Security. He stopped directly in front of her, his legs astride, his hands pushing back his gray suit jacket and resting loosely on his hips, his whole stance designed to intimidate. "All right. Now that we've started our week with a little chuckle, Miss . . ." He glanced down at her card. "Miss Ann Brentwood, Security Consultant . . ."

"Annie Brentwood," she corrected him. "The card says Annie. It's what I prefer to be called. Not Ann." Annie wished she could sound more sensible, but she was still in shock. One look at

Matt Harper, and she'd felt as if somebody had spiked her morning Gatorade.

"Atta girl," Victoria Harper said encouragingly. "Don't let him bully you."

Annie dragged her gaze from the impressive son to the equally impressive mother. Tall and regal, Houston's most prominent matriarch was blessed with the kind of good looks that only improved with age. She looked as energetic as she was beautiful in a brilliant sapphire linen dress that matched her eyes and complemented her salt-and-pepper hair. From her first glimpse of Victoria Harper, Annie had reacted exactly the way she'd always reacted to her own dauntingly lovely mother. But somehow Victoria didn't make her feel inadequate, and the woman's obvious support was a welcome surprise, so Annie grinned. "Don't worry, Mrs. Harper," she said cheerfully. "I'm hard to intimidate."

"I'm glad to hear it, Miss Brentwood," Victoria said with a smile. "Now, Matthew, be fair. What do you really think? Looking at the situation from a slightly different angle, don't you see the possibilities?"

He said nothing. He circled Annie, looking her over as if she were up for auction.

As his scrutiny went on, Annie lifted her chin even higher and gave herself a brief pep talk. She wasn't about to let some *nouveau riche* cowpoke in Italian loafers and an Armani suit bother her. She refused to be unnerved by his broad-shouldered stature or by his commanding aura. She did have to admit, however, that there was something disconcerting about Matt Harper—perhaps as ridiculously basic as the scent he exuded. Soap, she mused. Not expensive cologne. Just soap. It conjured up a vision of an outdoor shower on a spring day, of his bronzed, muscular, naked body streaming with warm water and fragrant lather. Annie's knees went weak.

Be critical, she hastily told herself. Hypercritical. There had to be something unattractive about the man. His features were rather rawboned, weren't they? Didn't he look as if he'd waded into a few saloon brawls?

The trouble was, he also looked as if he'd won every battle, with his maddeningly intact square jaw, chiseled nose, and prominent cheekbones. Annie figured he had a mean right hook, and, dammit, she did admire a mean right hook.

Even her fingers betrayed her, tingling with eagerness just because Matt Harper's light brown, gold-streaked hair was so touchable. Annie lowered her gaze, but got tripped up by his firm mouth. Her pulse flipped and her own mouth went dry. She moistened her lips with her tongue, deciding she'd better recapture a frayed thread of her professionalism before she became completely unraveled. She had to take control. Squaring her shoulders, she finally met Matt Harper's blue-green gaze. Within seconds she knew she'd made a mistake. She felt as if she'd just been knocked back through the swinging doors of his favorite saloon to land flat on her back, blinking up at the stars.

Come on, Annie, she told herself desperately. *Get out of the wild, wild west. Put on your mental fedora and think Bogie. Be cool.* With a supreme effort, she summoned a smile of pure bravado and faced those aqua eyes again. "Nobody sends for Sam Spade anymore, Mr. Harper," she informed him in her best tough-guy manner.

"The last Maltese Falcon flapped into the sunset years ago. Times have changed, and I can take care of any job Mr. Spade might have handled."

Matt suppressed a smile of amusement, at the same time battling the onslaught of sensations that had hit him anew when Annie Brentwood's eyes had started feasting unabashedly on him and she'd licked her lips as if she were a predator contemplating a light lunch. "Wrong, Miss Brentwood," he said, his voice slightly hoarse. He cleared his throat before going on; it didn't help. "You can't take care of this job. What possessed Charlie to send you? Why didn't he come himself?"

"The sandbags are too heavy," Annie shot back, then wished she had more self-control. Being nervous always made her cheeky. And she had to admit it—she was nervous, not only because of Matt Harper's impact on her senses, but because she needed this assignment. She took a deep breath and tried again. "Charlie treated himself to a ski weekend in the Rockies and slalomed into a sequoia, so he's flat on his back with his leg hoisted in the air, collecting autographs on his cast and giggles from pretty nurses."

"And you work for Charlie?"

"No, I work for myself. I'm a freelancer. I've done jobs for Charlie before, so—"

"What jobs?" Matt interrupted. "Finding lost budgies?"

Annie laughed good-naturedly and couldn't resist a bit of verbal sparring. "Budgies are somebody else's department. I'm Charlie's one-and-a-half-story man. I stand on his shoulders to peek over transoms."

Matt choked back a laugh, sent a fierce glance

toward his chuckling mother, then managed to frown at Annie. "Let's skip the cute cracks. What sort of jobs have you taken care of for Dunhill?"

"All kinds," Annie replied. "As I started to say, Charlie called me late last night and asked me to come over here this morning to keep his appointment. I juggled my schedule to fit you in. But don't thank me; it was nothing."

Matt narrowed his eyes at her. "Thank you for making time for us in your busy day, Miss Brentwood," he said with exaggerated politeness, then decided to put the woman in her place. "You certainly are a pert little thing."

Annie hesitated. The Texas accent always threw her. Had she heard right? "What did you say?" she asked at last. "Did you actually call me a purty little thing?"

"Pert," Matt repeated, doing his best to ignore Victoria's continuing mirth. "I said you were pert, not purty." His forehead creased in a flustered frown. "I mean, I'm not saying you're not purty— pretty—" He cursed under his breath, then cleared his throat. "I said *pert.*"

"Pert," Annie repeated, her lips twitching.

"As in impertinent," Matt added. But the word meant something else entirely to him as he took in the saucy swing of Annie Brentwood's dark hair, the upward sweep of the thick lashes that framed her eyes—her whole manner. Even her unusual voice, intriguingly husky, with an accent that was easy on the ears despite not being Texan, was part of the whole impudent package.

Suddenly he was assaulted by an unbidden image of the womanly curves under her clothing. Pert breasts, he thought before he could stop himself. A pert little bottom.

Sexy, he mused, then wished that particular word hadn't come to mind. Impertinent was safer. "Dammit, you can't do this job!"

"My goodness, what on earth is it?" Annie asked, taken aback. "An investigation into an oil-leasing company in some Middle East backwater where a female in business is about as welcome as a paper cut in a pickle factory?"

This time Matt couldn't help joining his mother in a burst of laughter at the girl's odd turn of phrase, but he quickly pulled himself together and tried again to get control of the conversation. "Was Charlie out of it on pain pills or something when he called you?"

"Charlie didn't know why we wanted him this time," Victoria belatedly explained. "I called the agency and asked him to drop by for a chat. I certainly didn't wish to discuss our situation over the phone."

Matt raked his fingers through his hair, curbing his impatience. It would have helped, he thought, if Victoria had provided that detail sooner. Turning to Annie again, he smiled apologetically. "What my mother actually wanted Charlie Dunhill for was bodyguard duty, not a routine business investigation. I'm sorry you came here on a wild-goose chase."

Annie shot a concerned glance at the older woman. "Are you in danger, Mrs. Harper? Are you worried about your personal security for some reason?"

"No," Matt said before his mother could answer. "Victoria's worried about *my* personal security. *My* body is the one she wants guarded, Miss Brentwood. Do you still think you're up to the assignment?"

Stifling a comment about how she'd love to give it her best effort, Annie scolded herself for her lechery, while wondering what had happened to the prude she'd always been. "Yes, I'm up to the assignment," she said, remembering something more important than her previously dormant libido: the need to come up with a sizeable chunk of money, fast.

"A real live *Charlie's Angel*, are you?" Matt drawled.

"Well, I'm not the kind of *Charlie's Angel* you mean," Annie pointed out, smiling. "I don't carry a gun, though I know how to handle one. And I don't go around saying *freeze* to drug barons and kidnappers."

"Then what *do* you do, Miss Brentwood?" Matt asked with sudden impatience. "Or is that information classified?"

Annie scowled, her good humor disappearing. He didn't have to bite her head off. "Look, Mr. Harper, I usually don't take much bodyguard duty. I graduated beyond that level some time ago. But I promised Charlie I'd cover this case for him because he doesn't have anybody else available, what with his accident putting him out of action just when everybody on his staff is tied up on some other assignment." Annie forced herself to smile again. The client was always right, she reminded herself. "I understand your reservations, but you have nothing to worry about. I can take care of you."

Matt gaped at her, then cupped his hand under her elbow and guided her to a mirror in one corner of the large office. "Look at us," he said, pointing to their reflection, his voice still thick with inexplicable desire. "Do you expect me to take you seriously?"

Annie was having trouble taking anything seriously. Her insides had started performing flips and pirouettes the instant Matt Harper had touched her, and looking into the mirror at the two of them standing side by side wasn't doing much to settle her down. To her horror, she kept imagining him turning, putting his powerful arms around her, and bending his head to capture her mouth with his. Fat chance, she thought. That sort of thing didn't happen to her. Nor did she want it to. "It's pretty ludicrous, I have to admit," she said with a shaky grin.

Matt nodded, satisfied that he'd made his point, and decided to ignore the way she had heated his blood and sent it coursing wildly through his veins with the force of a brushfire. He would be gracious, he told himself. He would even offer the lady a sort of consolation prize, a promise that she could hope for a more suitable assignment with Harper Industries another time. He opened his mouth to speak.

"However," Annie went on before Matt got out a single word, "I'd like to hear a few more specifics. I don't believe in refusing a case right off the bat, especially when I've promised to look into it." She turned away from the mirror to face him directly.

Matt's eyebrows shot up like two inverted vees as he stared down at her. "You don't believe in . . ." He was determined to stay calm. "Miss Brentwood," he said carefully, this time in a slightly strangled tone, "I'm not offering you the chance to turn down the job. If I'm going to give in to the demands of that woman over there—

who has been charged with the responsibility for hiring someone to protect me, even though she herself is the greatest threat to my life, limb, and sanity—I want a qualified watchdog. You are not qualified. Holler sexism if you like, but there are some cases where it's justified."

"Matthew, I can't believe my ears!" Victoria said sharply. "Are you the same man who initiated most of this company's well-publicized affirmative action policies? Or is equal opportunity fine as long as you don't have to deal with it personally? You'll be lucky if Miss Brentwood *doesn't* holler sexism, loud and clear!"

Annie tilted her head to one side and smiled. "Did I say a word about sexism? Did I even hint at it?"

Matt scowled. "You must have implied it, because that's what this nonsense is really all about, isn't it? This insistence that you can replace Charlie Dunhill?"

"If you want the real truth, Mr. Harper, what it's about is the temporary knot in my cash flow," Annie blurted out, her control stretched to the limit. "I don't have time to change the world; I'm just out to pay my bills. I study fingerprints, not gender roles." She paused for a breath, trying to bite her tongue. But the words had a will of their own; they simply tumbled out. "And the last thing I need," Annie heard from her treacherous lips, "is to put up with some Gucci cowboy who doesn't understand that real protection takes brains, not chest-thumping or duels at high noon. If you're in danger and whoever's threatening you gets so close that you need a gorilla to run interference, King Kong hasn't done his job." As she saw Harper's shocked expression, Annie closed her mouth, did a quick mental review of her incredible outburst, and made a fast decision before he could make it for her. "Sorry," she said, smiling and thrusting out her hand to grip his in a let-bygones-be-bygones clasp, "but I've decided not to take the assignment. Perhaps another time."

Matt was speechless as Annie Brentwood released his hand, stuck her nose in the air, and headed for the door.

"Don't you dare leave, Miss Brentwood," Victoria said, getting to her feet and drawing herself up to her full height.

Annie stopped in her tracks. Telling Matt Harper where to get off was one thing, but to defy a mother was another matter altogether. "You have a question, Mrs. Harper?" she said politely, turning to face the woman.

Victoria smiled. "Several. Please come and sit down." She moved toward a sitting area with a black leather couch and chairs, a white sheepskin area rug on the pearl-gray carpet, and a futuristically designed, smoked-glass coffee table.

Rousing himself from his stupor, Matt strode back to his desk. "Look, Mother—"

"Victoria," she corrected him pleasantly, then smiled at Annie. "We like to keep things businesslike at the office, but sometimes sonny here forgets. Won't you have a seat, Miss Brentwood? I'm sorry you've been kept standing so long. How about some coffee?" She turned her smile on her son. "Matthew, be a dear, will you?"

His jaw dropped. "You want me to serve *coffee*?"

Though Annie's glance moved back and forth between the two Harpers, she didn't budge.

To her astonishment, Matt tipped back his head and laughed, then went to the bar against one wall of the sitting area. "What the hell, why not?" he said, setting out large but fine white porcelain mugs and filling them from the carafe on the coffeemaker at one end of the shiny black counter. "You'd better sit down, Miss Brentwood," he added, still chuckling. "Otherwise our Queen of the Cowboys will get out her lasso and hog-tie you. She wants answers."

"Thank you, Matthew," Victoria said with a cool smile.

After serving the coffee, Matt settled himself onto the couch, took one of the cups, and leaned back, his foot propped up on one knee. He seemed to be preparing to watch a show.

Victoria raised a brow at him. "Now, I trust I'll be able to chat with Miss Brentwood without interference?"

"Victoria, did Dad ever turn you over his knee the way he always threatened to?" Matt asked idly.

To Annie's amazement, Victoria's lips curved in a small, dreamy smile before she remembered herself and glared at Matt. "That's none of your business. Now, Miss Brentwood, will you *please* come and sit down?"

Annie finally moved toward a chair and perched on it gingerly, refusing to sink into the deep cushions; she wanted to be ready to make a quick exit.

"Cream and sugar?" Victoria asked pleasantly.

Annie shook her head, not sure what to expect next.

"You take it black?" Matt asked, smiling. "So

does Victoria. I guess it suits the hard-boiled image."

Annie turned a pleading look toward Matt's mother. "Mrs. Harper, there's nothing to be gained by talking. I don't mean to be rude, but I must tell you that if I did take the job of protecting your son, my biggest problem would be refraining from doing away with him myself."

Victoria sighed heavily. "I understand perfectly. Matthew can be frustrating, Miss . . . May I call you Annie?"

"Of course. But—"

"Could you elaborate on what you said earlier?" Victoria cut in. "That business about gorillas and such."

Financial woes notwithstanding, Annie no longer wanted this assignment, but she couldn't see any harm in answering briefly. "It's simply that the smart thing to do is get to the source of the problem before there's a crisis. I could explain better if I knew a few details about this particular situation." Dammit, she thought, why had she asked? She didn't want any details. What she wanted to do was leave. On the double. "However, since I'm not—"

"I've gotten a few crank letters in the mail," Matt cut in. "I don't know why there has to be so much fuss about an occasional anonymous note."

"Occasional!" Victoria exploded. "Crank letters! Matthew, your casual attitude is all very sophisticated, but it's downright idiotic." She took a sip of coffee, then spoke quietly to Annie. "The hate mail started arriving a few weeks ago. Matt chooses to laugh it off, but I found even the earliest letters chilling, though all they did was mention one or two places he'd been just before the date at the top of the letter. No threats. Just a comment about a restaurant he'd gone to for dinner or perhaps a query about whether he liked the movie he'd seen."

Annie was getting caught up in the mystery. "Tracking his movements and letting him know he was being observed and followed. Have you talked to the police?"

"There's not much the authorities can do at this stage," Victoria said. "But the implication of menace is obvious, and lately there have been blunt threats, so I refuse to go along with Matthew's nonchalance any longer. And the other members of the family—who also happen to form a good part of this company's board of directors—unanimously agree. We took a vote. Matt lost. He gets a bodyguard-investigator whether he likes it or not, and I'm to do the hiring."

"Those letters are the ravings of some nut, that's all," Matt muttered into his cup.

"Perhaps so," Annie agreed. "But human filberts who write nasty notes have been known to crack and carry out their threats. Have you any idea who might be behind these letters? An archrival in business? Some woman scorned, perhaps?"

"My son scorns precious few women," Victoria said with a scathing glance his way. "But I'm sure he has disappointed many a young lady who wanted more from him than he's prepared to offer. Marriage, for example. A fourth date, for heaven's sake! His attention span seems to be limited to three encounters per woman. So even though there might be some merit in your suggestion of a business rival, I'm inclined to suspect that Love-'Em-and-Leave-'Em Harper has a version of *Fatal Attraction* on his hands."

Annie was listening only vaguely. Love-'Em-and-Leave-'Em Harper, she repeated silently, envisioning him squiring an endless succession of beauty queens. All of a sudden she felt depressed. Ridiculous, she told herself. Childish. But she stayed depressed.

"Do you agree, Miss Brentwood?" she heard him ask.

She looked blankly at him for a long moment. "Agree?" she said at last.

"With the *Fatal Attraction* theory," he explained, his eyes dancing with amusement. "Is some madwoman going to attack me for not asking her out a fourth time?"

Annie was horrified by the emotions racing through her and suddenly felt desperate to distance herself from the man. "It's difficult to say," she answered, resorting to textbook formality as she went on in a strained voice. "Are the letters perfumed or otherwise suggestive of a feminine hand?"

"Not necessarily," Matt answered. "I couldn't say whether the notes were written by a man or a woman, an acquaintance or a total stranger. Maybe you could if you saw them, Miss Brentwood, what with being a detective and all."

His every word was laced with irony, and Annie had to resist an adolescent urge to make a face at him.

"Matthew, so help me . . ." Victoria put down her coffee cup, took a deep breath, and smiled again at Annie. "Tell me, just how would you go about finding out who the sender is?"

Annie abruptly decided it was time to do a disappearing act worthy of the Great Zambini. "I really think you should discuss the problem with the investigator you hire. I suggest you explain things to Charlie so he can send someone Mr. Harper can feel comfortable with." She drained her cup and set it down on the coffee table.

"So you're leaving us to our own devices?" Victoria asked dramatically. "What if we can't find a good bodyguard? What if something happens to Matthew? Would you be able to live with his blood on your hands?"

Annie allowed herself a smile as she grabbed her purse, drew the strap over her shoulder, and started to get up. "I'd try my level best, ma'am."

"Poor Charlie," Victoria said with a theatrical sigh. "I suppose a detective agency is like any business. It's impossible to find help you can rely on."

Annie stopped halfway to a standing position and sank back onto her chair. "As I mentioned earlier, I don't work for Dunhill Security," she said evenly. She didn't like to boast, but she had more to lose by allowing herself to have her professionalism maligned than by speaking up and setting these people straight. "I'm not Charlie's hired help. I'm an independent consultant, specializing in business security."

"Interesting," Matt said lazily. "Care to explain?"

Annie glared at him. "All right, let me give you a few examples. You have a computer virus? I'll refer you to the best doctors to take the bark out of your bytes. Your alarm system is outdated? I can tell you whether it's upgradable or just degradable, and I know which experts can fine-tune all your bells and whistles. I've worked on industrial espionage cases, zeroed in on black knights plotting hostile-takeover bids, and caught a couple of white-collar embezzlers. I've done the down-and-dirty assignments, including my share of repos, missing-person searches, and seamy divorce stakeouts, and I've tailed a few plaintiffs in suspicious whiplash lawsuits to see if their neck braces are zippered for easy removal, but I don't need to be anybody's hired goon, even as a favor to Charlie. He'll be disappointed that this particular job wasn't for me, but he'll understand. He wouldn't have called me in the first place if he'd known what you were looking for."

"Bravo!" Matt said with a grin, wondering what Annie would say if he were to ask her to have dinner with him. Even her refusal would be worth hearing; he liked the way she talked, as if she'd read too much Raymond Chandler and watched too many shamus movies.

"You stay out of this, Matthew," Victoria said, then turned back to Annie. "My dear, I disagree. I think you're absolutely right for this job. Don't ask me why; it's just an instinct."

"Woman's intuition," Matt said teasingly.

"Exactly," Victoria retorted.

Annie stood up. This time, she vowed, she was going to leave. "I'm sorry, Mrs. Harper, but I don't believe in intuition, at least not as some psychic phenomenon. Perhaps as a combination of concentration, observation, logic . . ."

"A logical woman?" Matt put in, adding a derisive snort for good measure."

Annie turned to go. She'd had enough.

"A logical woman. Now that's what I call a classic oxymoron," Matt murmured, not sure why he was still baiting Annie. She was leaving, wasn't she? Didn't he want her to go?

"*Who's* a moron?" Annie demanded, whirling on him.

"Not moron. Oxymoron. As in self-contradictory."

"I know what an oxymoron is," Annie said, slightly mollified. "I didn't hear you, that's all." Then she realized that what he'd said was as insulting as what she'd thought he'd said. She also noticed that he was grinning, as if he knew how badly he'd rattled her. "I have to go now." She turned again to make a fast beeline for the door. "I do believe I've had my fill of masculine charm." Over her shoulder, she gave Matt a saccharine smile. "Another oxymoron, wouldn't you agree?" She knew she'd hit home when her target gave a low whistle of surprised appreciation.

"Annie," Victoria said too sweetly, "please explain to poor Charlie that we'll have to take our considerable business to another agency from now on. We simply can't deal with a firm whose representatives leave us in the lurch."

Annie turned very slowly. "Not fair, Mrs. Harper."

Victoria smiled, nodded, and sipped her coffee.

"It's blackmail," Annie protested.

"We have an ongoing contract with Dunhill Security," Victoria said. "Either it's honored, or it's broken."

Matt glowered at his mother. "Victoria, cut it out, for Pete's sake. Miss Brentwood knows she can't handle the case."

"The hell I can't," Annie snapped before she remembered that the last thing she wanted was this job.

"Then it's settled," Victoria said, putting down her coffee cup with a solid clunk that was like a punctuation mark. She got up, strode past Annie, and opened the door. "Come to my office now and we'll get you started."

Matt rolled his eyes in frustration. "Annie, don't let my mother buffalo you. I won't let her give Charlie the heave-ho for circumstances beyond his control."

"Oh really?" Victoria drawled. "Have you forgotten the vote the board took? Come along with me, Annie. You're going to protect my son's hide, as worthless as it might be."

As Victoria swept out of the office, Annie gave Matt a feeble smile and stood still for a long moment, her knees too wobbly to be trusted. They'd developed a tremor when he'd used her first name. It was an awful feeling. Terrifying. "I'll go with your mother," she said quietly, "but only to explain once and for all that this arrangement won't work. I'm sure I'll make her see reason."

Matt shook his head. "Trying to make Victoria see reason is like trying to talk sense to a tornado, Miss Brentwood. Once she whirls into action there's no stopping her. But let me assure you, vote or no vote, we won't dump Charlie if you beg off this job. I have the right of veto, and even though I use it sparingly, this is one bluff Victoria won't be able to follow through on."

Annoyingly disappointed that he'd reverted to her last name, Annie gave him a tight little smile. "Don't worry, Mr. Harper," she said as she walked toward the door. "I don't want this assignment any more than you want me to have it. Your mother isn't going to change my mind, and that's that."

The last thing Annie heard as she followed in Victoria's wake was Matt Harper's infuriating, know-it-all laughter.

Two

Victoria Harper's office was slightly larger than her son's and every bit as sleek and functional, her choice of bright colors the only concession to traditional femininity.

Annie smiled to herself. What had she expected? Overstuffed chintz and daisy bouquets? The aroma of baking cookies? From what she'd seen so far, Victoria was about as traditionally feminine as a marine drill instructor.

"Make yourself comfortable," Victoria said, leading Annie to the sitting area. "We have some nitty-gritty decisions to get out of the way. First, I assume that you can start right away and that you're free to devote all your time and attention to my son's well-being?"

What an awful prospect, Annie mused, glad she'd decided not to be talked into the job. Settling into an armchair upholstered in silky-soft raspberry leather, she met Victoria Harper's steady gaze. "There's something you simply have to understand, ma'am. Without your son's cooperation, nobody can give him proper protection. There has to be an enormous amount of confidence, trust, and comfort between a client and a bodyguard. And let's face it: Matt Harper might have confidence in a sumo wrestler with a .44 magnum in one hand and a bowie knife in the other, but not in a five-foot-five lady packing a laptop computer in her shoulder holster."

Victoria laughed. "Actually, Matthew would make life miserable for any security person. And it occurs to me that an obvious bodyguard isn't a good idea if we want this letter writer to come out in the open. Even Charlie wouldn't have been the best choice for this job. You are."

Annie shook her head. "I don't see why."

"You would if you weren't smarting because Matthew wounded your pride," Victoria said smoothly. "But let me explain: We'll present you as his special assistant—a consultant to help him with a particularly tricky acquisition he's just starting to work on. You'll stay close to him without anyone being the wiser about your real purpose. You'll observe every person he encounters, business acquaintance . . . and otherwise."

Annie's determination to refuse hardened. "You're looking for physical, around-the-clock protection? From me?"

Victoria mulled that one over for a few moments. "It's my understanding that you *can* provide physical protection, Annie, despite your comments about packing a computer instead of a weapon. Am I wrong?"

"Well no, but—"

"I'll be brutally honest," Victoria interrupted. "I think the latest letters suggest that some sort of crisis is coming very soon. And let's go back to my pet theory. What if this person is an obsessed female who hasn't struck yet simply because Matt hasn't spent enough time with any one young lady to trigger a jealous rage? Having you close to Matt, very publicly close to him, could smoke her out."

"I thought I was supposed to be your son's special assistant, not his special . . . well, girlfriend," Annie said, telling herself she was speaking academically, since she intended to refuse the job.

"But if you're with Matthew day and night, the logical assumption will be that you're special in both ways," Victoria responded without hesitation.

The woman had the whole scenario planned out, Annie thought. "So you want a decoy, not a bodyguard or an investigator."

"I want a decoy, yes," Victoria answered. "But also a bodyguard and an investigator. You *could* carry a weapon, couldn't you?"

"I have a registered handgun and I know how to use it, but I'm not into playing Billy The Kid. Honestly. I'm a pacifist. And you must see the obvious complications hiring me would cause."

"Then suggest someone, Annie. Someone more qualified than you to replace Charlie."

Annie's teeth worried her lower lip. Charlie had told her that all his top staff people were tied up on assignments, and she knew who was available at other agencies. The pickings were slim at the moment. Modesty aside, she was the only competent person she could think of. Yet she resisted taking the job, and didn't blame Matt for not wanting her to be hired. What bachelor would want a lady private eye posing as his lover and creating awkward problems with his actual women friends? And given his effect on her, did she want to be hanging around on the sidelines while Matt Harper romanced some . . . some drum majorette? "No!" she blurted. "Twenty-four hours a day keeping an eye on that man? I can't. I won't even try. Sorry. It's impossible."

Victoria sighed. "I suppose it's a lot to ask. But you wouldn't be working all the time. You'd just be on call. During the day, when Matthew is safely tied up in his office, you could slip out for shopping or dentist appointments or whatever. You'd have your own office here—I've already set one aside for Charlie—so you could run your investigation and even take care of other client calls if you wished. After hours, you'd be eating, sleeping, often just relaxing—I hope you can abide a steady TV diet the likes of *Andy of Mayberry*, or whatever it's called. The point is you'd be close to Matthew in case the need arose."

"Mrs. Harper, it's too ridiculous!" Annie exploded. "Have you looked at your son lately? He's a one-man platoon! If he'd been at the Alamo, Davy Crockett might have ended up as president of Mexico! Your Matthew makes John Wayne look like a sissy, and you're saying he needs *me* to protect him?"

Victoria nodded, a soulful expression in her eyes. "Yes, Annie. That's exactly what I'm saying. Matthew seems to think he's invincible, but the rest of us in the company and in the family know better. He's so accessible. He's like a friendly puppy, for heaven's sake. Anyone could walk right up and shoot or stab or do heaven knows what to him. You could keep something terrible from happening, Annie. You know you could. Now, about your fee—"

"Money isn't the issue," Annie put in, scowling. To her surprise, the fee had become the very least of her concerns. "Charlie already told me what you pay him. It's a regular cash-flow dam-buster, but it isn't the point."

"Well, just for the record, dear, I'd planned to offer double the usual hourly rate for this job. And since you'd be on call for twenty-four hours a day, you'd be paid for twenty-four hours."

Annie stared in shock. "What?" she repeated in a small voice. All at once she saw her fiscal problems drifting away. She saw her defecting partner's intense relief at getting a buy-out check. She saw her own bank account growing instead of disappearing. She saw herself leaving Texas in a few months and going back East where she belonged. "Did you say double? For twenty-four-hour days?"

"Of course," Victoria answered almost impatiently. "Would you expect less, considering the nature and the importance of the assignment?"

Annie let herself dream for a moment, then forced herself to stop. What mattered wasn't money, but her inability to do the job. She had all the necessary skills, but she questioned her effectiveness under the circumstances. And in the long run, nothing else mattered. "Mrs. Harper, I—"

"Wait, Annie," Victoria interrupted. "Please remember that we're talking about my son, not about some information leak or faulty alarm switch. I truly believe you'll put everything you've got into finding out who's stalking Matthew and why. Call it a hunch, but I'm a good judge of people, and I don't think very much gets past you, Annie. You're bright, you're observant, you're gutsy." Victoria grinned, her eyes twinkling with sudden humor. "Now, you may have noticed Matthew feels protection is being foisted upon him.

He'll be annoyed that I've hired you over his objections, and he'll want to send you packing. But he won't be able to, thanks to my cooperative board of directors."

"He says he has the right of veto," Annie pointed out.

Victoria arched her brow. "Oh, he managed to tell you about that little technicality, did he? Well, it's true, but it's nothing for you to be concerned about. Matthew is bullheaded, but he respects the decision of the majority and he's never overruled me. If I say you're his bodyguard, he'll abide by my choice." She smiled. "But he'll launch a campaign to get you to quit. He'll do everything in his power to send you running back to Charlie, admitting you couldn't hack it. He's already started. And judging by your reluctance to take the assignment, he's succeeding admirably."

"I didn't say I was reluctant," Annie protested. "I just wanted to be sure . . ." What was she saying?

Victoria's eyes widened with sudden hope. "So you'll take the job?"

Annie slowly wagged her head from side to side, trying to say no. But the raw plea in Victoria's expression got to her; she simply couldn't turn her back on a mother who was frightened for her son, even if that son was a rangy, arrogant, disturbingly virile Texan. "I'll take the job," she heard herself agreeing at last.

"And you won't let Matt push you into quitting?"

Annie grimaced. "I won't let him push me into anything," she said, then sighed heavily, wondering exactly what she'd let herself in for.

*   *   *

Within the hour, an office close to Matt's had been set up for Annie on the top floor of the gilded glass tower that was headquarters for Harper Industries.

She had a huge desk, a desktop computer, and a comfortable swivel chair in the butter-soft leather the Harpers seemed to favor. She also had a sweeping view of fountains and parks and more of the ubiquitous glass towers in the downtown core of the city that always amazed her with its unrelenting newness.

For some reason, Annie thought as she glanced around her spacious, gray-carpeted office, she'd expected a cubbyhole. She smiled. How foolish. A cubbyhole? In Texas?

Victoria had offered her a secretary of her own, pulled out of the office pool, but Annie had refused. A personal secretary would catch on that she was a detective, not a special assistant, and the fewer people who knew, the better.

Annie didn't feel like much of a detective at this point. She couldn't figure out something as fundamental as who was really boss of Harper Industries. She didn't know much about the company at all, for that matter. According to the sketchy information Charlie had given her over the phone the previous night, Victoria had taken control of Harper Industries ten years before, immediately after the death of her husband, Owen, who'd built the company on a foundation of oil, ranching, and real estate holdings. Matt had joined the firm four years later at the age of twenty-five, and was responsible for an aggressive expansion into retailing, publishing, and electronics. Charlie said Victoria was still head honcho, but Annie wasn't so sure.

Telling herself that the internal problems of the Harper family were none of her concern, she began going through the anonymous letters. She was interrupted after only a moment by a tap on her open door, then a deep voice. "I gather you made my mother look reason straight in the eye, Miss Brentwood."

"Let's say Victoria's arguments to get me to sign on were more persuasive than mine to beg off," she said, slowly looking up and smiling calmly despite the sudden racing of her pulse. "It seems that you and I are going to have to stick together like peanut butter and jelly for the next little while, Mr. Harper."

Matt didn't find the prospect of being sandwiched with Annie Brentwood too unpalatable, and he'd expected it to happen. Very few people were a match for his mother. Nevertheless, the stark fact of the matter was that Annie had allied herself with Victoria against him in the dumbest plan he'd ever heard, and he had no intention of making the woman's life easy. Besides, the more he thought about Annie Brentwood, the more he wanted to know her—but not professionally. He wondered how long it would take for her to decide the job was more trouble than it was worth. Not long at all, he promised himself. "I gather you're to be introduced as my special assistant, parachuted in for the negotiations with Milton Software. What expertise are you supposed to be bringing to the project?" he asked with feigned earnestness.

Annie hadn't thought that far ahead; she'd assumed Victoria would fill in the details of her cover. Suspecting, however, that her slightest hesitation would give Matt ammunition for his battle to oust her, Annie made a quick decision and smiled. "I'm something of a computer hack. If you're thinking of buying a software company, you're probably taking a close look at its products. Who knows? I might actually be helpful to you."

Matt couldn't help grinning. Annie was going to be a worthwhile opponent in this battle of wills. He would win, of course. He didn't believe in losing; even his formidable mother and the posse of relatives and loyal henchmen she called a board of directors could push him only so far. "By the way," he went on, "Victoria tells me you're prepared to do twenty-four-hour duty, Miss Brentwood. Does this mean you're moving in with me?"

"I guess it does, unless you'd prefer to bunk in at my bachelorette walk-up," Annie answered evenly. But her imagination and her body conspired to betray her. The prospect of keeping an eye—a very close eye—on Matt Harper day and night suddenly hit her with such vividness, she felt a hot, crimson blush spreading over her skin. She concentrated on controlling her breathing. It didn't work. She got to her feet and went to the file cabinet against the far right wall, hoping she'd hidden her face soon enough so Matt couldn't guess what was happening to her. She opened a drawer and pretended to look for something in the still-empty folders.

Matt was watching Annie too intently to miss the color flagging her delicate cheekbones, and before she'd gotten up and turned her back on him he'd seen coppery flames flare up in the depths of her dark brown eyes. All at once the voltage in the air was crackling almost audibly, and intense erotic awareness was filling the room. Twenty-four hours a day, he thought as desire pulsed through him with startling speed and power. He *had* to get Annie off the job, he told himself again. "Look, I realize freelancing can be difficult, especially in your field," he said gravely, pacing the room. "I could steer you to plenty of other clients . . ."

"I didn't accept this case because I need clients," Annie retorted, slamming the drawer shut as she whirled to face him. She frowned as her glance followed his agitated strides. "Sure, I can use the assignment, and the pay your mother has offered is terrific, but I've taken you on strictly because Victoria believes I'm up to the job and I *know* I'm up to it. If you're as eager to be rid of me as you seem, try being helpful. Somebody's sending you nasty notes, Mr. Harper. That somebody could be about as dangerous as Bambi, but we don't know for certain. The only intelligent thing to do is find out who your pen pal is. The sooner we nail him or her, the sooner I'll be out of your hair. All right?"

It wasn't all right, Matt thought. He didn't want Annie out of his hair. Just off the payroll. Off his Forbidden Females list. Besides, if there was a genuine threat to him in those letters, he wasn't about to hide behind her sleek little skirt.

For the moment, though, he masked his determination with bland pleasantness. "Hey, I didn't mean to ruffle your feathers, Miss Brentwood," he said with a forced smile. "I'm sure you *are* up to the job. And you're right. The smartest course is for me to cooperate with you to find out who this weirdo is. So tell me what to do."

Annie eyed him warily, not trusting his sudden change. But she sat down and returned his smile, pretending to go along with his peace offering. "Thank you, Mr. Harper. Right now I need some time to go over the letters. Perhaps later we'll have something to discuss."

"I'm sure we will," he said, then couldn't resist winking at Annie as he left her office. "In fact, I know we will."

Annie stared after him for several moments, suspecting that war had been declared.

She turned her attention back to the letters. In an effort to ease into concentrating on them properly, she glanced through the envelopes. All of them were the standard business size, all post-marked Houston, no letterhead or return address, naturally. Not much to go on there, Annie thought. She began a close study of each letter.

They'd all been typed on the same typewriter, an old one with several characters badly worn, the lines uneven, as if the roller wasn't holding the paper tightly enough.

She checked the dates and read the letters in chronological order. By the time she'd finished the latest ones, she was utterly perplexed. *You've got a lot to answer for,* one note said. *Start praying, Harper.* Annie couldn't imagine why Matt doubted that a crisis was on the way. If he was laughing off this kind of thing, he was the very worst sort of client to protect.

After going over and over each line of every letter again, Annie still hadn't found any solid leads. She wasn't surprised; no job was that easy.

There was another tap on her open door, and Annie looked up, realizing with surprise that she'd been lost in her work for almost an hour.

Matt's attractive blond secretary was standing in the doorway. "Sorry to interrupt, Miss Brentwood," Josette Nicholson said in the honeyed tones of a native southerner.

Annie smiled. It was her envious opinion that the descendants of the Confederate States of America could say anything from the trite to the outrageous and make it sound sweet and playful, all because of their delightful drawl. "No problem," she said, her glance taking in the younger woman in a quick assessment, including the girl's ring finger. "And please call me Annie." She'd already met Josette, but hadn't paid much attention. Now she had reason to be more observant.

By Annie's educated guess, Josette was barely twenty. She was also violet-eyed, unforgivably pretty, and single. Annie wondered about the boss-secretary relationship—for investigative purposes only, she hastily told herself. It didn't matter to her in the least if Matt Harper chose to rob the cradle and chase his secretary around the desk, unless those antics led to anonymous letters.

Realizing that the scrutiny was mutual, Annie lifted her chin. "Is there something I can do for you?" she asked as politely as she could manage.

Josette blinked, seeming to emerge from deep thought. "Matt asked if you'd come to his office," she said with a smile, then added as Annie got up to follow her, "but I warn you, he and Victoria are goin' at it like a couple of bobcats over a possum, and I somehow get the feelin' that the possum in question is you."

Annie couldn't help laughing, though she wasn't sure how she felt about being called a possum, and she didn't look forward to another session with the Harper bobcats.

"Don't you worry, though," Josette said as they approached Matt's door. "I doubt if you're on the carpet already, you havin' just started this mornin'. But if you are, take my advice: Stand up to those two. Laugh the way you did a second ago. It's the only way to handle 'em, and you've got a real nice little chuckle there. I'll bet it makes Matt smile just to hear it."

I'll bet, Annie said silently, musing that Josette was moving rapidly to the bottom of the list of suspects. Of course, she was the only one on the list so far. "Wish me luck," Annie said as Josette opened Matt's door and stood back to let her enter the inner sanctum.

Victoria was sitting on the couch with her arms folded over her chest, her expression unreadable. Matt was at his desk, leaning back in his chair, his hands laced behind his head. Another man was perched on the corner of Matt's desk, sporting a muscle-bound body under his tight T-shirt.

"Miss Brentwod, I have good news for you," Matt said, grinning in a way that immediately got her hackles up. "There's no further need for your services after all. I phoned the neighborhood gym. This gentleman, who was kind enough to come right over, is Mervyn McAllister. I'm sure you'll agree just by looking at Mervyn that he's well-equipped to be my bodyguard."

Annie surveyed Mervyn. A supercilious smile tilted up his thick lips. An amateur, she decided. And a smug amateur at that. "I see," she said quietly. "And the investigative aspect of the case? I trust your gymnasium teaches those skills along with bench-pressing?"

Mervyn McAllister chuckled and shook his head. "So you're the little lady who likes to play the tough private eye. Wait'll the guys in the locker room get a load of this!"

Annie smiled sweetly. "How nice. I've always wished I were the kind of gal a fella would talk about in a locker room." As McAllister digested that comment, she turned and speared Matt with a look that almost made him wince. "Mr. Harper, it's your life, so you do what you wish, but if somebody knifes you in the back, I'll show up at your funeral just to lean into your coffin and whisper I told you so."

McAllister stood up as if to display his massiveness. "Honey, nobody's gonna knife nobody while Big Merv is on the job," he said with a superior smile. "Now why don't you go sharpen some pencils? Better still, find yourself a real good man—"

"Annie," Matt broke in. He was glad his gimmick had worked, but he wished the gym manager had sent over someone with a little more class. "Thank you, Miss Brentwood," he said, his smile strained. "Thanks for being willing to take on the case, and for being so reasonable about giving it up."

In her corner, Victoria said calmly, "You work for Harper Industries, Annie, not for Matt Harper. And the chief of Harper Industries has not asked you to resign."

Annie looked at Victoria and shrugged. "I'm sorry, but what can I do when I'm faced with reality?"

Matt smiled, though he was slightly surprised and oddly disappointed that Annie had given in so easily. "You'll be reimbursed generously for your time and trouble, Miss Brentwood," he said politely. He stood, walked around the desk, and thrust out his hand to her. "No hard feelings?"

Nodding, Annie accepted the handshake. "None whatsoever, Mr. Harper," she said, telling herself that if she'd needed any proof that she shouldn't have taken this assignment in the first place, she had it in the warmth that coursed through her at the mere touch of Matt Harper's hand—and, she thought as she looked down, in the way he wasn't releasing hers.

Matt followed her gaze and realized he hadn't let Annie go. He found, to his surprise, that he didn't *want* to let her go. But he didn't like being forced into anything, and he'd been forced into accepting her as his so-called bodyguard. As a matter of principle, she had to go. Besides, he'd twigged to his mother's real reason for being stubborn about hiring Annie, and he wasn't at all happy about using her to lure some basket-case enemy of his out into the open. Then there was his personal interest. He intended to call Annie as soon as there'd been time for her inevitable resentment to fade. He realized it could be a while. Clearly she wasn't pleased that he'd decided to replace her. The copper flames that had excited him since he'd first looked into her eyes had been joined by icy shards of anger. It was fascinating, he mused, how two opposing emotions could coexist in those dark, shimmering depths. "It's been a pleasure getting to know you," he said in a low voice as he finally released her hand. "I'll—"

"Yeah," Big Merv said, reaching out to claim a handshake of his own, his large paw enveloping Annie's hand and his fingers crushing hers in a clumsily blatant effort to prove his strength once and for all. "A pleasure, lady. But get out of the bodyguard business. It's no work for little girls."

The man had locked Annie's hand in his grasp, just as she'd expected he would; her response was automatic. She spun her body into his, using the momentum to gain leverage, and the lummox shouted in surprise as he jackknifed over her shoulder.

She smiled down at Big Merv as he lay sprawled on his back on the soft carpet, his eyes blank with shock, and she was thoroughly pleased with herself. She glanced at Victoria and winked.

Victoria's eyes were sparkling, but otherwise her expression remained impassive.

Annie glanced guiltily at Matt and wished she had a camera to catch his astonished expression. "I'm so sorry," she said without a shred of sincerity, then tried to appear concerned as she looked down at Big Merv again. "But really, Mr. McAllister, shouldn't you be more alert?"

He glared at her. "Hey, that's not fair. I didn't know you wuz gonna pull that kind of trick!"

"True," Annie agreed with mock sympathy. "Unfortunately, attackers rarely warn their victims. Perhaps you should keep that fact in mind in the future—for Mr. Harper's sake, as well as your own."

"Matthew," Victoria said, sounding bored as she got to her feet. "Have we had enough of this farce yet?"

For a moment, Matt didn't answer. He was too busy battling a compelling urge to haul Annie Brentwood into his arms, insanely glad she'd defeated him. "It seems, Merv, that we've underestimated Miss Brentwood," he said at last, struggling to keep a quiver of amusement out of his voice as he helped the large man to his feet. "I guess you're the one who'll be reimbursed for the time you've already put in. Thanks for coming over. Rest assured we'll call on you should we need your kind of muscle in the future."

"What happened to fair play, anyhow?" Merv muttered. "I'm goin' back to wrestlin' with the guys at the gym. At least in the ring you know what's gonna happen next." He mumbled all the way out of Matt's office, covering a range of complaints from "uppity women" to "broken rules" and a world where you couldn't "trust nobody no more."

Annie resisted the urge to ask him to give the boys in the locker room her best.

Matt flashed Annie a sheepish grin. "Okay, let me have it. Say your piece, Miss Brentwood."

Victoria shook her head. "Matthew, why don't you apologize properly and let Annie get back to the job of preserving your miserable neck?"

Annie jutted out her jaw. "I'm not sure Annie's willing to get back to that particular project."

"And I'm not sure Annie should," Matt shot back, suddenly more determined than ever to oust her. In the past few minutes she'd fired his simmering desire for her to the boiling point. And she'd made him like her too much to take even a slight chance of putting her in danger for his sake. She had to go—but in a way that wouldn't make her hate him. "Annie, let's talk," he said quietly.

"Annie, beware of this boy," Victoria put in. "So far Matthew has attempted sarcasm and bullying, even to the point of bringing in reinforcements. Now he'll trowel on the charm. Are you going to fall for his boyish sincerity, or are you going to remember your promise to me and show him what you're made of?"

Matt felt a powerful urge to steer his mother out the door, lock it behind her, and find out in his own way what Annie was made of. He suspected there was a lot more sugar and spice and all things nice than Annie seemed ready to admit. But he'd been brought up to be a gentleman, at least of sorts, so he remained quiet and let Annie make her own decision.

Ultimately, however, Annie didn't make the decision. Her body made it for her. Her throat closed over when she tried to say she was giving up the case after all. Her legs refused to move an inch until she silently agreed not to direct them out of the Harper Industries building. And as she gazed into Matt Harper's bottomless aquamarine eyes, the common-sense cells of her brain simply cut out, as if somebody had pulled the plug to their power source. Besides, she *had* promised Victoria she wouldn't let Matt make her quit. She was stuck.

"Fine," Victoria said at last, beaming. "Now we can all get back to work. Come along, Annie. You have a would-be assassin to catch"—she smiled over her shoulder at her son—"and someone, best described by a shorter form of that word, to protect."

Three

Professional curiosity eventually got the best of Annie. She got down to work on the puzzle of the letter writer's identity, going at the problem from a new angle.

She began sifting through the press clippings she'd requested from the company's public relations department. Once again she was so absorbed in her work, she didn't notice the time whizzing by, and she actually jumped when the now-familiar voice said, "Ready, Miss Brentwood?"

She looked up and frowned, annoyed that she'd let Matt Harper know he'd startled her. "Ready for what?"

Matt smiled. "For lunch," he said with mock innocence.

"Lunch?" Annie repeated blankly.

"Lunch. The noon meal. Do you have a different name for it back in . . . Where do you come from, anyway?"

"Massachusetts," Annie said.

Matt nodded, not surprised. "I figured as much. What brought you all the way to Texas?"

She wasn't sure how to answer. She certainly didn't want to go into a recital of the chain of mistakes and foolish decisions that had landed her in Houston a little more than a year before. "Let's just say I'm like Ulysses," she answered distractedly.

"You mean like the Greek hero, off on some personal odyssey?"

She smiled. "No. I mean like the James Joyce book. Banned in Boston."

Matt was intrigued. "Why? Did you get into some kind of trouble there?"

"Actually, I was kidding," Annie said, wishing she'd said something less provocative.

"No you weren't," Matt argued. He moved to her desk, perched on the corner of it and grinned down at her.

"Of course I was kidding."

"No you weren't," Matt said stubbornly. "It's your family, right? They don't approve of your profession."

"I was *joking*!" Annie insisted, wondering how he'd managed to zoom straight in on the truth so quickly. "Okay, my folks probably wish I were more like Bettina and Amy. . . ."

"Who are Bettina and Amy?"

"My sisters. I'm the middle daughter, and I admit I'm the family's little black lamb. Bettina's two years older, married to a doctor, mother of two perfect children. Amy's five years younger, single, just out of college, beginning a teaching career that she'll quit as soon as she marries her lawyer fiancé."

"And how old are you, Annie?"

Her frown deepened. "I don't think you have the right to ask that particular question, but I'll answer just to be civil. I'm twenty-six. How old are you?"

"Thirty-one," Matt answered with a chuckle. "And thanks for being so civil. It's heartwarming, that's what it is. Now, back to the Annie Brentwood saga. Where were we? Your folks don't approve of your career, and maybe they're not too sure what to make of *you*. They're prim Bostonians, are they? Ancestors came over on the Mayflower?"

Annie laughed and her eyes danced with fun. "Heavens, no! Grandfather Brentwood always swore that our ancestors arrived on the *second* boat, after having sent the family servants ahead to Plymouth Rock to tidy up the place a bit."

Matt let out a low whistle. "So we're talking real American bluebloods. No wonder you were banished."

"I wasn't banished!" Annie protested. "My folks aren't *that* rigid."

"Then something else drove you from Boston," Matt said thoughtfully. "Let's see what kind of detective I'd make. You left home because in the course of a routine case you stumbled onto something big, something that could earn you a place in Boston Harbor with all the tea that's been steeping there for a couple of centuries. You came to Texas because nobody would look for you here."

"What a fertile imagination you have, Mr. Harper," Annie said, laughing. "But you're a terrible detective. I left Boston because I wanted a change."

"Why Texas?" he asked. "Isn't your job difficult enough without trying to do it in one of the last American bastions of macho privilege?"

Annie couldn't help grinning. He was so right. "I was working at an alarm-system firm in Boston when my feet started to quiver," she explained. "A colleague of mine was feeling the same way and suggested we strike out on our own as free-lance consultants. We picked Houston because she already had a line on a company here that needed a major report on its various security needs. We pooled our savings, set up an office, and won the contract."

"So you have a partner," Matt said thoughtfully. "I suppose she's looking after the rest of your clients while you take care of me."

"Actually, Cheryl—Cheryl Wilson, my *former* partner—met the cowboy of her dreams two months ago. He's a struggling rancher, and he says he needs his wife home on the range, so I have to . . . Cheryl has left the business. She's asked me to buy her out." Annie was annoyed by her slip. She didn't like letting it be known even in a small way that she felt let down by her former partner, forced into a tight financial corner by Cheryl's change of heart just as things started going well.

But Matt had noticed Annie's quick correction. He knew the buy-out must have created problems—such as the knot she'd mentioned in her cash flow. "By the time Cheryl pulled out, I guess you'd fallen in love with Texas and decided to stay," he said casually.

Annie gave a short burst of laughter, as if he'd made the most ridiculous remark she'd ever heard. "I'd go back East in a minute. Maybe not to Boston, but certainly to New York, or even Philadelphia. Unfortunately, Cheryl and I locked ourselves into a two-year lease on our office, so I'm stuck here for another eleven months, one week, and four days."

Matt studied her intently, astonished by the bleak feeling he was experiencing at the thought of her leaving Texas. It was insane. Didn't make any sense at all. "The whole situation sounds pretty unfair to me," he said, trying to ignore his eccentric emotions. "You're talking about being stuck in a place you're obviously not too fond of, simply because you've committed yourself to a lease. Yet this Cheryl walked away from the lease and her deal with you. Why should you be left holding the bag?"

"Cheryl didn't know she was going to get hog-tied and branded," Annie said defensively. She knew that a good businessperson wouldn't let Cheryl off the hook at the cost of almost sinking the fledgling company, but she understood Cheryl's predicament. "What was the woman supposed to do?" she went on when Matt gave her a raised-eyebrow look that suggested her gray matter was short a wrinkle or two. "Should Cheryl have waved good-bye to her true love as he rode off into the sunset without her, all for the sake of a business she'd discovered she wasn't that excited about?"

"There's such a thing as honoring a commitment," Matt insisted, not sure why he was so troubled by Annie's predicament—or why his would-be bodyguard was arousing his protective instincts.

"Ah," Annie said. He'd given her the perfect opening to make a point. "I couldn't agree more, Mr. Harper. And I plan to honor my commitment to your mother to do my level best to find out who's playing a sick version of post office with you. So perhaps I should get back to work."

Matt got up and walked around the desk to look

over her shoulder at the papers she'd been study-ing. Press clippings, he mused. Good idea. Per-haps somewhere in one of them there might be a hint of a business enemy he'd managed to make without being aware of it. "But the most import-ant part of your job, as I understand it from Queen Victoria, is baby-sitting me," he reminded Annie. "And I'd like to go for lunch now, so you have to tag along."

She couldn't speak for a moment. Matt's taut thighs and lean hips were almost touching her upper arm as he stood looking over her shoulder, and his impact on her senses was mind-numb-ing. "I . . . I suppose you're right," she finally said, a slight tremor in her voice.

Matt recognized Annie's response to him. The sudden excitement emanating from her was tan-gible—and arousing. "Of course I'm right," he said softly, forgetting about press clippings and intentions and rules as he bent down to lean his elbow on the desk, pretending to be taking a closer look at a newspaper story, but in fact want-ing to be closer to Annie. She was like a powerful magnet he couldn't seem to resist. He turned his head to smile at her, losing himself again in her dark, expressive eyes.

Annie swallowed hard and told herself he was trying a new brand of intimidation—a highly effective brand. She was having trouble breath-ing. She couldn't think. All she could do was focus on his mouth, suddenly so close to hers, the warmth of his breath caressing her skin, the penetrating intensity of his gaze stripping away the thin veneer of her professional reserve. "Right about what?" she asked blankly, losing track of the conversation.

"About everything," he murmured. "About lunch, about you taking on this case . . . and about . . ." He faltered, all his attention now on Annie's soft, generous lips.

Feeling the tips of her breasts hardening, Annie was glad she'd kept her jacket on. But her ragged, shallow breathing was impossible to hide. "And about something else?" she prompted, praying he would straighten up and leave, yet wishing crazily that he would end the aching suspense and take her mouth in a searing kiss instead of merely gazing at it as if considering the possibility.

Matt was too shocked by his own feelings to think clearly. He'd known countless beautiful, exciting, sexy women. Not one of them had affected him with the erotic power of this one. What was the matter with him? Spring fever? "About lunch," he murmured.

"You already said that," Annie whispered.

He kept looking hungrily at her mouth. "Already said what?"

Annie was beginning to consider taking matters into her own hands, twining her arms around the man's neck, and kissing him. He was so tempting.

As Matt saw Annie's lips part slightly and sensed the barely perceptible softening of her body, he was gripped by a wild urge to cover her mouth with his and crush her body against him. But a minuscule part of his brain was still operative. It remembered his rules. Lunch, he repeated silently. He was going to spend the noon hour trying to get this woman out of his office and into his private life. "C'mon, Annie," he said huskily. "What kind of bodyguard are you? Where I go, you go. Peanut butter and jelly, you said."

"Oh," Annie whispered. Her mouth was dry. Instinctively, she moistened her lips with her tongue.

"Oh, is right," Matt said raspily, a coil of raw desire twisting inside him.

"Maybe . . . maybe I'd do more good staying here going through the files," she managed to say.

"It's a little late to concentrate on damage control," Matt argued in a low, persuasive voice, trying to remember that he was talking about his phantom enemy and not his body's wild response to her. "Let's face it," he added teasingly. "I could be shot during the soup course, and it'd be all your fault."

Annie swallowed hard. "Blackmail," she whispered. "Like mother, like son. Next you'll be asking whether I could live with your blood on my hands."

"Could you?" he murmured.

Annie tried to muster a smart-aleck retort, but couldn't seem to think of one. She was in a trance, focused completely on Matt's firm, sensual mouth, almost feeling it moving over hers. Gentle, she thought vaguely. He would be gentle. His kiss would be sweet and evocative. It would leave her aching for more . . .

Matt's lips were just touching Annie's when he stiffened and pulled back, staring in genuine shock at her. He was appalled by what he'd almost done. Had he lost his mind? Or was he just intoxicated by her sweet, feminine scent? Mesmerized by those fatal eyes? Captivated by her husky voice and pixieish charm?

Straightening up, he frowned and raked his splayed fingers through his hair. "I'm sorry, Annie.

I didn't come in here with the intention . . . What I mean is, I don't . . ." He hesitated again, still shocked. "I don't believe in mixing business with pleasure," he said, more to himself than to her, as if he needed a firm reminder.

Annie wasn't sure what to think. Had he been toying with her? Was he out to prove a point? Using the charm Victoria had warned about? She'd never seen a man look as confused or as vulnerable as Matt Harper did at this moment.

But she had to be mistaken. Matt Harper, vulnerable? Was she out of her mind?

She managed a smile. She had to try to defuse the situation by making light of it. "So much for the appetizer, Mr. Harper. Shall we go somewhere more public for the rest of the meal?"

Annie gave Matt's plate a baleful glance as the waiter brought their main course. "You know, the universe is divided into two clearly opposed camps," she commented, trying to ease the charged atmosphere that had existed since he'd almost kissed her. "There are liver haters and liver lovers."

"Which are you?" Matt asked, though he already knew. Annie's obvious distaste for the dish, expressed by her wrinkled-up nose when she'd seen it on the restaurant's list of daily specials, had been his reason for ordering it. He was going to be merciless about making her job untenable in every way he could think of. Especially after that near-kiss. He'd never lost control of himself that way before. "Which, Annie? A liver lover or a liver hater?"

Annie merely made an eloquent face.

"That's too bad. You won't enjoy your first duty, then." Matt smiled benignly as he stabbed a small chunk of liver with his fork and reached across the table to hold it close to her mouth.

She averted her face. "No thanks. My mother tried for years to get me to taste the stuff and never succeeded. You're not likely to do better. Besides, what organ meats do to a person's cholesterol count proves that Mom was wrong for once. They're *not* good for me. What duty?"

"To taste my food, of course. Don't you have to make certain it's not poisoned?"

Annie stifled a laugh. "Good idea," she said after a moment. Steeling herself, she let Matt poke the loathsome morsel between her barely parted lips and tried to pretend it was breaded and badly spiced chopped steak. But all she could think of was a disgusting blob rolled in sawdust and tossed in a greasy pan until it turned muddy brown. An eternity seemed to pass before she managed to swallow the thing, and for all her self-control, she couldn't suppress a shiver of distaste.

Shaken by the heat that had swept through him as he'd concentrated on Annie's parting lips, Matt smiled with a mischievous satisfaction he didn't feel. "Now, are you going to tell me that wasn't the most delectable delicacy ever to tickle your taste buds?" he managed to say. "How about some more? Some onions?"

Annie shuddered again, picked up her tumbler of water, and drained it. "There's no need for me to have another taste," she said primly. "I believe you can go ahead and safely eat your lunch."

"Good," Matt said, tucking into his supposedly favorite dish. She was game, he had to admit.

Annie Brentwood was going to give him a battle royal. Fine. His ultimate victory would be that much more satisfying.

Annie waited until he'd savored several bites with lip-smacking enjoyment, then murmured, "By the way, it did seem poisoned to me."

He shot Annie a look of mock horror and let his fork clatter to his plate. "You said I could eat it!"

"Why, so I did," Annie answered with a smile. "What a silly goose I am, making a mistake like that!" She shrugged. "Oh well. Everybody's entitled to one slip-up, right?"

Matt laughed appreciatively. The woman was a minx. And she seemed to have no idea how alluring she was. Deciding it was better not to dwell on Annie's sexiness, Matt motioned to the waiter and ordered a new meal for himself. He was grateful for the excuse. He hated liver. "Go ahead with your salad, Miss Brentwood," he said after the waiter was gone. "My burger plate special will be here any minute."

Automatically putting down her fork, her strict manners too deeply ingrained to let her nibble away until her lunch partner was served, Annie glared at him. "So you don't like liver any more than I do, Mr. Harper," she said, realizing with wicked satisfaction that he'd choked down a lot more of it than she had, all the while pretending he was doing it with gusto. "You were testing me," she went on, then decided to indulge in some Harper-style theatrics. Clutching her throat, she widened her eyes. "Dear heaven, what if that food *had* been laced with arsenic or cyanide? I could be dead by now! And my very last sensation would have been that sickening slab of worn-down saddle leather! Have you no conscience, Mr.

Harper?" She touched the back of her hand to her forehead melodramatically.

"It would be pretty difficult for somebody to poison a restaurant meal of mine," Matt said calmly, getting a kick out of Annie's act. "I have no regular lunch spot. I've never tried this particular dining room before. But I admit I was testing you, and I'll go on testing you until you tell me to take this job and—"

"I'd have to say it to your mother, not you," Annie cut in. "Victoria's the one who hired me, remember?"

"Of course she did. Mother's happy to enlist an extra ally for the Harper petticoat tyranny."

Annie couldn't hold back a burst of laughter, though Matt's remark confirmed her suspicions about a family rift. "Petticoat tyranny? What a quaint term."

"Right. Quaint," Matt said with exaggerated disgust. Suddenly he remembered why he preferred to keep females from getting too close to him. He had enough women in his life. "There are four of them," he muttered.

"Four what?"

"Four women, not counting you. My mother and my three older sisters."

Annie laughed again. *Older* sisters, she mused. Was Matt a long way down on the power totem pole? Or had his gender automatically placed him at the top? The dynamics in this family could be interesting to observe—preferably from afar. "So there are three junior versions of Victoria at home? And in the company?"

"Scary thought, isn't it?" Matt said, out of habit masking his profound affection. "They're not exactly at home, though, and they haven't chosen to be involved actively with the company except on the board of directors."

"Good grief, are you ruled by a board made up of Victoria and your sisters?" Annie asked with genuine sympathy.

"There are others," Matt admitted. "A brother-in-law, a couple of retired Harper executives, a family friend who's been a major stockholder for years."

"What do your sisters do? Why aren't they working for the family firm?"

"Mirella's a fashion designer living in Dallas with her husband and four kids; Adrienne and her husband are travel writers, so they're always on the go; and Felicia's a cellist with a symphony orchestra, married to the first violinist; they're on tour half the time. But there are regular visits to the family ranch, and by some weird coincidence or built-in rhythm, everyone usually lands there at once. All hell breaks loose, let me tell you."

If the other Harpers were like Victoria and Matt, Annie thought, she could imagine the bedlam. But something else Matt had said intrigued her. "Mirella, Adrienne, Felicia," she repeated. "What great names. How I envy your sisters."

Matt smiled, oddly touched by the wistfulness in Annie's tone. "Personally, I think yours is a nice name. It's . . . well, it's sweet. Unpretentious. An Annie is someone a person can feel comfortable with."

"A buddy," she supplied with a resigned grin, wondering why she felt a stab of disappointment at finding that Matt Harper, like most men, was comfortable with her. Just once, she thought, just once she'd like to make some male uncomfortable. "An Annie is the kind of female a fellow can talk to about his passion for all those Mirellas and Adriennes and Felicias," she commented cheerfully, remembering that she herself cultivated her good-pal image, though she wasn't sure why. Her career wasn't the only reason; she'd been accepted into boys' tree-house clubs from the time she'd been old enough to climb up to them.

Folding his arms on the table, Matt leaned toward Annie and slowly wagged his head from side to side. "I'm not buying your sad tale, Miss Brentwood." He allowed himself a leisurely visual tour of her touchable hair, her soft skin, her inviting mouth. "I'm prepared to believe you used to be a first-class tomboy, but if you think men still see you as a pal—or a potential buddy—you're missing the signals."

Annie was transfixed. If the look in Matt Harper's darkening blue eyes was the kind of signal he was talking about, she didn't see how she could miss it. At the moment she didn't feel like a buddy, a pal, or a tomboy. She felt like a woman. A desirable woman. And a very nervous woman. She wasn't supposed to be a desirable woman. She was supposed to be a private cop.

Suddenly she remembered Matt's bluntly stated purpose: to make her turn in her badge. And she'd almost fallen for his act. "Speaking of friends," she said with renewed determination, "we have to discuss yours."

Matt was amazed by Annie's sudden transformation. The softness in her eyes had been banished with a blink, replaced by stubborn defiance. He realized what she was thinking, and he felt like throttling his mother for planting the suspicion that he would use seduction as a weapon.

His own mother! Didn't she know him better than that? And couldn't Annie see her effect on him? So now she wanted to discuss the women in his life, he thought disgustedly. "Forget it," he answered abruptly. "I don't kiss and tell."

"And I don't especially want to hear about your Don Juan exploits," Annie snapped, then wished she had a better grip on herself. She tried again. "As you know, Mr. Harper, your mother seems to think—"

"Victoria doesn't know what she's talking about," Matt said sharply. "We're not dealing with the fury of a woman scorned here, Miss Brentwood, or even a woman miffed. Nobody I go out with expects to domesticate me. I don't lead any ladies to believe I'm interested in becoming a lapdog."

"A lapdog? Is that what you think happens to a man just because he's mature enough to . . . ?" Annie took a deep breath. Matt Harper's views on relationships were irrelevant. Yet she couldn't seem to curb her tongue. "From what I've seen," she said evenly, "if the human male is turned into a pooch on a leash, he's more likely to be Jaws the Pit Bull than Benji the Benign."

Matt forgot his defensiveness and laughed, disarmed again by Annie's turn of phrase. He was grateful to the waiter for choosing that moment to deliver his burger plate. Being with Annie was like sparring in a boxing ring; every once in a while a little rest between rounds was welcome.

Annie was silent until the waiter was gone, then returned to the main point. "You know as well as I do that ladies sometimes get ideas of their own about what's happening in a relationship. A woman can lead *herself* on, often with little encouragement. She can get so caught up in a romantic spell, she doesn't realize that the picket-fenced cottage dancing in her head is, in the mind of Mr. Wonderful, nothing more than a water bed at the Whoopee Motel."

Matt cocked one eyebrow with sudden interest. "Did he hurt you that badly, Annie?"

Annie stared in horror. Was the man a mind reader? Not that she'd ever been dumb enough to be lured into a motel—though she had let down her guard on occasion. But good lord, it had been three years since she'd woven fanciful dreams around any man. She hadn't allowed any of that silliness since the time she'd seen David Harrington smiling sexily at her across a crowded room.

Nowadays she was amused by the monumental naïveté that had put stars in her eyes on that occasion. David's only interest in her had been wangling an introduction to her father. And why not? Carter Brentwood was an influential man, and David hadn't been the first ambitious Young Turk to attempt to get to her father through her; he'd simply been the first who'd succeeded in breaching her outer defenses. Fortunately, she'd realized her mistake before she'd made a complete fool of herself. David had remained blissfully ignorant of the oceans of tears she'd shed on his account.

Yet Matt Harper knew. Or suspected. The man was scary.

Matt frowned, sorry he'd blurted out a comment that had hit a nerve. And something else bothered him: If he didn't know better, he might believe he was jealous of the man Annie was thinking about at the moment. "Annie?" he asked gently.

She came out of her reverie with a start. "We're

not discussing me, Mr. Harper," she said in clipped syllables. "We're discussing you. I don't see how you can be sure you haven't led any woman on."

"If I have, it wasn't done on purpose, so it's the lady's own problem," he insisted, picking up his hamburger and chomping into it ferociously.

Annie gave a loud sigh of exasperation as she began pushing lettuce leaves around on her plate. "Mr. Harper, it's *your* problem if a woman is demented enough to fall so hard for you that she'd write those letters."

Matt chewed thoughtfully for a moment, realizing he was glad to see Annie's feistiness again. Her faraway expression had bothered him. "You think a woman has to be demented to fall for me?"

"I think a woman has to be demented to stay in the same room with you!" she shot back. "Are you going to take this situation seriously, or are you going to keeping playing court jester? Either way is fine with me; I'm being paid for my time, and the clock's ticking."

Relenting, Matt nodded. "Okay. I'll get serious. I'll tell you why I'm so sure those letters aren't from any woman I've gone out with."

Annie braced herself, though she wasn't sure for what.

Matt saw the sudden set of her jaw, the straightening of her shoulders. It pleased him that Annie didn't enjoy asking these questions any more than he liked answering them. "What you have to understand," he said carefully, "is that I deliberately stick to a certain kind of woman. She's invariably attractive, of course. . . ."

"Of course," Annie couldn't help muttering as

she ruthlessly impaled an innocent cherry tomato on her fork.

Matt paused, then grinned, shrugged, and went on. "She's as independent as I am, not looking for permanent ties, just out for a few laughs."

Annie rolled her eyes in disdain. "Ha!"

"Ha?" Matt repeated. "That's an interesting editorial comment. What does it mean, exactly?"

"Are you kidding? Do you honestly believe that those cool kittens are for real? Don't you realize they're just smart enough to know how to attract you? What do you expect an interested female to do, anyway? Haul you into her father's library and have him ask you to state your intentions? I'll probably have to check out every last one of your . . . your paramours!"

Matt feigned innocent surprise. "You mean every woman I so much as take to dinner is out to put her brand on me?"

"Of course. How can you be so gullible?"

He put on an aw-shucks grin. "I just didn't know I was so all-fired desirable, Miz Brentwood. I'm sure glad you've warned me. So these ladies are playin' hard to get?"

Annie scowled. His good-ol'-boy drawl certainly had thickened all of a sudden. "Probably," she murmured.

"Is that what you're doin', ma'am?" he asked. "Playin' hard to get, I mean? Because you sure are convincin'. A minute ago you said any woman who came near me had to be deranged—"

"Demented!" Annie said, flustered.

"And now you're suggestin' that to know me is to love me," he continued. "It's confusin', ma'am, it surely is."

Annie balled her hands into fists in her lap and

silently counted to ten. He was having fun with her, she reminded herself. She'd been warned by his mother that he would do his level best to upset her into retreating, and that his flirtatious, mercurial moods were all part of his campaign.

It wasn't going to work, Annie told herself. She wouldn't let it work.

When she felt reasonably calm, she smiled and batted her lashes at him. "You're too clever for me, Mr. Harper," she said in the most syrupy tones her Massachusetts accent would permit. "Why, you've seen right through my act. I've been trying to pretend I want to protect you from some shadowy enemy, when all along I'm really just angling for a proposal from the most devastating bachelor in Houston, maybe in all of Texas. But honestly now, aren't you a little bit tempted to escape the lonely tedium of bachelor life? Wouldn't you just love to find a bed to park your snake-stompers under permanently? Doesn't the scent of orange blossoms go straight to your head? Don't the sweet strains of a Lohengrin march and the echoes of wedding bells pierce your lonely heart? Haven't you longed for the pit-ter-pat of little—"

"All right, all right," Matt said, laughing and holding out both his hands in a desperate "stop" gesture. "You win. I'm getting a rash."

"And I'm getting tired of having every sentence I utter twisted into a semantic pretzel," Annie said brusquely. "I'd suggest we finish eating and get back to the office. I have work to do, especially since you don't seem to plan on giving me a whole lot of help."

Glancing at his watch, Matt was amazed how quickly time had zipped by. If he didn't hurry, he was going to be late for a meeting of the head office vice presidents. But he hated to see the lunch date end. It had been more fun than he'd had in a very long time.

Besides, he found himself wanting to know more about Annie Brentwood, to understand why such a lovely woman seemed to have so little regard for her own allure, to know what had caused that wistful look he'd seen when she'd lapsed into such deep thought.

And above all, to figure out why this imp excited him in ways he hadn't known he could be excited.

Four

By the end of the day, Annie had combed through all the press clippings of the past year and jotted down a number of names she wanted to discuss with either Matt or Victoria.

She decided she'd rather work with Victoria than Matt, and didn't care if she was being cowardly. Cowardice was a useful quality in certain circumstances, and spending too much time with Matt Harper was one of those circumstances. Besides, he hadn't shown much willingness to answer her questions so far; his mother would be much more helpful.

The phone rang just as Annie was reaching for it. She jumped slightly, then picked up the receiver.

"Annie," Victoria said.

Annie laughed with surprise. "I was just going to call you. I have some things I'd like to ask you, some notes to go over—"

"Tomorrow, dear. We'll go at your notes first thing in the morning. Right now I have to dash off to a museum committee meeting. I just wanted to wish you good luck this evening and reassure you that my son, for all his faults, is a gentleman.

You may not be comfortable with him, but you'll be safe. But for heaven's sake, don't fall for any of his tricks. Don't let him make you quit, Annie. You have backbone. Use it." The line went dead.

"Backbone," Annie muttered as she hung up. She'd managed all afternoon to avoid thinking about the evening ahead. Now she was face-to-face with it. "Brainbone is more like it."

"Who's a brainbone?"

Annie's head snapped up. "How long have you been standing there?"

Matt grinned as he leaned on the doorjamb, his hands in his pockets and one leg crossed over the other. "I just arrived. Who's a brainbone?"

"I am."

"Why?"

"Many reasons. What can I do for you, Mr. Harper?"

"It's quitting time," he answered cheerfully.

A seismographic tremor rippled through Annie like a warning of a major quake to come. "Quitting time?" she repeated in a small voice, wishing the man didn't dominate a room with his sheer physical magnetism.

"Quitting time, home time, whatever you call it in Boston," he went on, giving her a disgustingly dazzling smile. "But being the jelly to my peanut butter shouldn't spread your energies too thin, Miss Brentwood. Thanks to Charlie, I have an efficient alarm system at my apartment, so you can come on over, make yourself at home, and rest easy, knowing you're doing your duty but aren't likely to be called upon to save me from some stranger in the night."

Annie stared at him guardedly. Why was he being so good-natured?

Matt waited. When Annie didn't seem to be retreating from the prospect of spending the night at his place, he tried another small nudge. "You seem a mite subdued, Miss Brentwood. Will staying with me be a problem for you?"

"Well it's . . . it seems . . ." Annie wished she could strangle the man. He had her just where he wanted her. If she admitted she was edgy about staying in the same house with him, she would be admitting he should have held out for male protection. But if she went along with this insanity, she was asking for trouble she had no experience handling. That kiss—almost-kiss, anyway— might have been nothing more than a tactic on Matt's part, but it had lit a fuse to a cache of erotic explosives, a bomb she couldn't seem to dismantle. "Do you have enough room for me at your place, Mr. Harper?" she asked, wishing she could stop sounding like Snow White on helium.

Suppressing a mischievous grin, Matt gave a nonchalant shrug. "I live in a small apartment, but I'm sure we can fit you in somewhere," he answered.

A small apartment, Annie repeated silently as she tidied her desk, getting ready to go. How small? And how long would she have to spend closeted in a bachelor pad with the most devastating man she'd ever met, supposedly to defend him from an attacker? Her heartbeat went crazy. What if *she* turned out to be the attacker? Somehow she had to get out of this particular duty. "Aren't we carrying this charade a bit far?" she asked with a lift of her chin.

"I have no idea what you mean," Matt answered with exaggerated innocence.

Annie narrowed her eyes at him. "You just don't let up, do you!"

"No, ma'am, I don't," he admitted without hesitation, then stepped forward and flattened both palms on her desk as he leaned over it. "You want to play bodyguard, Miss Brentwood? Fine. We'll play bodyguard." Straightening up, he smiled again. "Shall we go?"

She began trembling with mingled excitement and anger. "Why are you so stubborn? Why are you so determined to get me off this case?"

"You're a detective, and you need something that obvious spelled out for you?" he asked, then pivoted on his heel and headed for the door.

Annie made a face at his back and jumped up to follow him, grabbing her purse on the way.

She realized she'd misinterpreted his intention—or he'd changed his mind—when he suddenly closed the door and wheeled around just in time for her to crash into him and drop her purse.

His arms went around her, strong and steadying. He stared at her for several long, charged seconds, then spoke roughly. "Okay, I *will* spell it out for you, Miss Brentwood. First, I don't believe there's any real threat behind those letters. Whoever wrote them is like an obscene phone caller, too chicken to come out in the open and actually do something. Second, if by some chance there *is* a threat, I don't want you in the line of fire. I'm not in the habit of asking anybody to fight my battles for me, least of all a delicate, lovely woman. And third . . ." He stopped, belatedly realizing that Annie was in his arms, gazing up at him with an expression of shock and unmistakable desire. "Third," he said, swallowing hard, telling

himself to push Annie away before he did something he would regret. "Third, I don't . . . I . . ."
Not quite sure how it happened, he found his lips
moving over hers, his willpower and scruples dissolving instantly, as if he were being drugged by
the sweet, hot taste of her.

Annie imagined she could hear Victoria's voice
in her conscience, ordering her to battle the lan-
guor overtaking her with alarming speed. She
couldn't. She tried to be outraged, but she wasn't
that much of a hypocrite. Matt hadn't intended
to kiss her any more than she'd intended to issue
a silent, eager invitation. She knew she was
wrong to respond, yet as the gentle pressure of
his mouth coaxed her lips apart, she opened to
him with unchecked eagerness, her tongue meeting his, stroking, dueling, exploring. She discovered a thirst only he could slake, a hunger only
he could satisfy. As his hands began moving over
her back, she twined her arms around his neck
and let him mold her contours to his hard planes.
His desire for her was real; Annie was sure of it,
and her certainty gave her a burst of feminine
power she'd never known before. Matt wanted
her. His heart was pounding with a violence that
couldn't be faked. The heat and rigidity of his
body as he pressed into her wasn't a lie or a trick.
Matt Harper wanted her as much as she wanted
him.

But all at once he was tearing himself away,
glaring down at her, his hands going to her
shoulders and curving around them to hold her
back, as if he had to defend himself against her.

Annie didn't know what to think. Why was he
looking at her with such horror?

"Annie," he said, his voice thick. He pulled her

hard against him again, buried his face in her hair, and groaned softly. "Annie, I didn't mean for that to happen. I swear I didn't. What *is* it about you? I can't seem to think clearly when you're around. I behave like a maniac! Can't you see how impossible this situation is? Annie, for crying out loud, will you give up this farce?"

"Farce?" Annie repeated. What exactly did he mean? The kiss? The desire they'd both felt—or at least that she'd felt?

Her body went rigid as she sucked in her breath, finally understanding. "It was a trick!" she cried, pushing him away.

Matt frowned and reached for her again.

Annie moved fast, stepping behind her chair and using it as a shield. "I had no idea how far you'd go to try to make me quit," she said in a wooden tone as she battled hot, stinging tears. When was she going to learn that she just wasn't the kind of woman a man lost his head over? "What's the problem, Mr. Harper? Is there more to this story than meets the eye? Are you worried I'll go poking through something you don't want me to see? Did Victoria really hire me to find out who's harassing you, or does she think you're up to no good, and she wants to know about it?"

"Don't be melodramatic," Matt said with a hoarse laugh. He bent and retrieved her handbag, then handed it to her. Another unreasonable female, he thought. Hadn't Annie started that kiss? Hadn't she catapulted into his arms? Even if it had been an accident, she hadn't tried too hard to move away. And the invitation in her eyes hadn't been his imagination.

Above all, Matt couldn't understand how Annie would think he'd been play-acting for the sake of achieving his purpose. Didn't the woman know anything about men? "I'm sorry to disappoint you, my suspicious little Sherlockette," he added, his voice vibrating with irony, "but there aren't any dark secrets here for you to unravel."

Annie wasn't so sure. But she was certain of one thing: Matt Harper had pushed her too far. Nothing except being fired by Victoria would make her back down now.

"Judging by the gleam of retribution in your eyes," Matt said carefully, "you'd like to launch a sexual harassment suit right about now." Not that he would blame her, he thought disgustedly.

"Don't be silly." Annie glowered at him. "We're both aware you could file a countersuit. I don't think I started that clinch, but I know I didn't stop it. Besides, I'm not big on taking my problems to court. I fight my own battles."

"So do I, Miss Brentwood," Matt shot back, grabbing any opportunity to drive home his point. He opened the door and made a courtly bow to let her precede him through it.

Annie gave him a baleful look and swept past him. "Not this battle, Mr. Harper," she said, her chin jutting out pugnaciously. "According to the lady who hired me, this particular battle happens to be mine."

"The parking attendant will put your car in the company garage," Matt said curtly as he and Annie rode down in the elevator. "You'll travel with me from now on."

"With any luck, it won't be for long. This is one case I want to solve in a hurry." She couldn't stop herself from adding another little jab. "In the meantime, I hope I won't cramp your style too much."

"No problem," Matt said, suppressing a perplexed frown. Annie sounded jealous. It was an
emotion he didn't care for, in himself or in the
women he associated with. Yet Annie's apparent
jealousy gave him an unexpected thrill. What was
this maddening female doing to him? "I managed
to break both dates I had for this evening," he
added, just for the pleasure of watching her jaw
clench.

Annie stiffened. "I'll need to stop by my apartment to pick up a few things," she said in her
most businesslike tone. "Some clothes, a tooth-
brush, the pearl-handled derringer I like to slip
into my satin garter."

"I hope you're joking," Matt interrupted.

Annie shrugged. "Okay, no satin garter."

He raised his brow disapprovingly. "And no
pearl-handled derringer, either."

"Of course not, but I do have my trusty automatic."

"No guns," Matt ordered softly.

Annie stared at him. "No guns?"

"No guns," he repeated. "I'll go along with this
foolishness, but not that far."

"What's wrong?" Annie demanded, getting her
back up. "Do you think I'll shoot you . . . or
myself in the foot?"

"Not at all. But Victoria told me about your
anti-gun sentiments. It's bad enough that you
were coerced into taking this job; I don't want or
need you to bend your principles on my account.
Besides, a gun in the hands of someone who's
reluctant to use it is worse than no gun at all."

"Are you sure you're a Texan?" Annie murmured half to herself, thunderstruck.

"Miss Brentwood, I'd have thought you were too

bright to fall for stereotypes," he scolded mildly. "But yes, I'm definitely a Texan. What I can't figure is why you'd try to set up shop as a detective in this state when you feel the way you do about weapons."

"I'm still trying to figure the same thing," she muttered.

As the elevator came to a stop on the ground floor and the doors slid open, Matt put his hand on the small of Annie's back to guide her toward the lobby's reception desk. He liked the way her body stiffened slightly. He was getting to her. Of course, she was getting to him, too, but that was beside the point. "In any case, there'll be no derringers, Berettas, or anything else that goes bang in the night," he went on firmly. "If that restriction bothers you—"

"It doesn't," Annie interrupted. On the contrary, she was pleased. "I told you I wanted to depend on my deductive skills to track down this poison-pen character, Mr. Harper. Your mother's insistence that I hover over you makes sense only . . ." Annie stopped. Perhaps Matt didn't know she was supposed to be a decoy to smoke out Victoria's theoretical crazy lady. She had a feeling he wouldn't take too kindly to the idea.

"Because what?" Matt prompted, scowling.

Annie thought fast. "Because she's a very worried lady," she told him.

They'd reached the large reception desk, and Matt held out his hand to Annie, palm up. "If you'll describe your car and give me your keys and license number, I'll leave them here for the parking attendant. He'll move it to an empty spot near mine."

As Annie dug into her purse for her car keys

and recited her license number, she noticed the attractive redheaded receptionist looking at her with acute interest. "An '88 Camaro," Annie added. "White. Row eight in the visitor area."

"Thanks, Tina," Matt said to the redhead as she put the keys in an envelope and wrote down the instructions. "If Marty doesn't come for the car before you leave, be sure to tell your night replacement where the keys are, will you?"

"Sure thing, Matt," Tina answered, giving him a quick smile, and then subjecting Annie to a thorough inspection.

A suspect, Annie decided. A receptionist who called a member of the company top brass by his first name and checked out his new special assistant as if sizing up the competition. Maybe Tina wanted to persuade Matt to break his rule against getting involved with employees. Or perhaps he'd already broken it but had been gripped by regrets afterward and was trying to ditch her now. Or maybe he'd just invented the rule after they'd kissed.

How revolting, she thought. Of all the clients to get involved with personally, why had she picked on the Houston Hotshot?

Matt discovered that he was beginning to read Annie enough to pique his curiosity, but not enough to know just what was going on in her mind. How, he wondered, should he interpret the sudden arching of her slender neck and the cocky tilt of her head, the lowering of her thick lashes to half-mast so they veiled the expression in her dark eyes? Was she being an observant detective or . . . something more personal?

He brought himself up short. What did he care? Any woman who didn't recognize raw male desire when she was literally up against it was too damned inexperienced for him. "See you tomorrow, Tina," he said, cupping his hand under Annie's elbow to steer her toward the building's main exit.

"If not sooner," Tina drawled, giving him a lazy smile.

Annie decided that Tina definitely had to be considered a suspect. The thought was depressing. Had there been an affair? Had Matt enjoyed his fun with Tina and then breezed on to his next conquest, figuring he could go back to the employer-employee relationship? Was Tina telling him, not very subtly, that she wouldn't stand for his cavalier attitude? That she expected him to join her later in the evening? Had her words, in fact, been an outright threat? "Do all your employees speak to you that way?" Annie asked Matt when they were outside.

"What way?" he asked, momentarily nonplussed.

Annie rolled her eyes. "Maybe you have something to tell me about Tina, Mr. Harper."

Matt scowled as he looked around, then muttered a curse as he realized what an idiotic thing he'd just done, thanks to the way Annie had rattled him. His car was in the garage, where it always was. Unless he wanted to walk all the way around the building to the ramp entrance, he and Annie had to go back inside and take the elevator. No wonder Tina had given him a funny look. "Come on," he said to Annie, choosing not to explain his absent-mindedness.

She followed him, thoroughly confused.

"Forget something?" Tina asked, her eyes dancing.

"You're fired," he muttered, striding past the amused receptionist toward the elevators.

Tina laughed. " 'Night, boss. Take it easy, huh?"

As Annie began to realize what had happened, and understood why Tina had made her earlier comment, she felt a little silly about overreacting to a teasing remark. Still, she had her doubts. Harper had gotten awfully addled talking to the receptionist. "As I said," she persisted once they were on the elevator, "do you have something to tell me about Tina?"

"Such as?" Matt asked, hardly paying attention.

"Look, Mr. Harper," Annie answered with exaggerated patience. "I realize that you Westerners are a lot less formal than the folks back home, but a receptionist kidding around with the company's big cheese, calling him by his first name? It's a bit much, isn't it?"

Matt stared blankly at Annie. "What's the problem?" he asked after a moment. "We *are* pretty informal around here."

"Is everyone on a first-name basis, then?" she asked stiffly.

"Pretty much," Matt answered. The elevator opened, and he steered Annie through the parking garage toward his car. "It started with my father; he wasn't one to stand on ceremony. The way Dad saw it, if you couldn't command respect without resorting to a lot of phony etiquette, you didn't deserve it. He liked a relaxed atmosphere, and so do my mother and I. Tina's a breezy type, that's all." He hesitated, then couldn't resist adding, "Why did she get under your skin so much?"

"She didn't. I have a job to do, remember? I have to question everything and wonder about everybody. And I certainly have to wonder why that lady gave me such a thorough eyeballing that she probably could tell you my measurements down to the last quarter inch."

Matt didn't bother saying he wouldn't need Tina to tell him Annie Brentwood's measurements. He knew the only thing that counted: Annie fit beautifully in his arms. "Tina is on the verge of getting an engagement ring from the guy she's been nuts about for two years, Miss Brentwood," he said evenly. "She's also the daughter of my first cousin. I think you can take her off your suspect list. Here's my car."

Annie was surprised as Matt opened the passenger door of a dark blue, midsize, late-model Buick. No flash at all.

Matt saw her puzzled frown. "Did you expect a block-long Caddie?"

"Or maybe a Corvette," she said, for some reason warmed by Matt's apparently genuine lack of pretension. "Before I get in, Mr. Harper, would you open the hood of your car?"

He cocked his head to one side and gave her a look that was so puzzled, Annie nearly laughed out loud.

"So I can check to make sure the vehicle isn't rigged," she explained.

"Rigged?"

"As in wired, Mr. Harper. Planted with enough plastic explosives to blow you to Brownsville as soon as you switch on the ignition."

Realizing what she was up to, Matt suddenly tipped back his head and roared with laughter.

Her hackles rose. "I won't get into this car until I've checked the engine. I'd prefer to have a mechanic put the vehicle on a hoist and give it a proper going-over, but I realize we have to make certain compromises for the sake of practicality."

"Be my guest," Matt said, moving to the driver's side to open the door, reach in, and pull the hood release.

Annie went to crouch down at the back of the car, making a production of checking the tailpipe. "I'm assuming it would be difficult for anyone to attach anything under the body in broad daylight and within clear view of the attendant's booth," she said as Matt stood back to watch her little show. "Everything seems fine here." Straightening up, she marched to the front of the car and peered under the hood.

Matt shook his head in amused admiration. "Do you really know what you're doing? What you're looking for?"

"Of course," Annie said smoothly, then reached up and closed the hood. "We're all set."

"And will we go through this act every time we want to use the car?"

Annie smiled and returned to the passenger side to climb in. "We will if I have anything to say about it."

Getting behind the wheel, Matt heaved a deep sigh. "Then I suppose we will," he said wearily. "As I've already said, I'm ruled by a petticoat tyranny. A mere male doesn't stand a chance."

Probably, she thought, it took the concerted efforts of four strong women to keep the buck in their midst from riding roughshod over all of them.

And that was one thing she was determined he wasn't going to do to Annie Brentwood.

* * *

Matt frowned as Annie used her building's tele-phone-style intercom to buzz her apartment. "Don't you have a key?" he asked, struck by an unpleas-ant thought: Perhaps Annie didn't live by herself.

"Of course I have a key," she answered. "But someone's staying with me at the moment, and I . . . Hi," she said into the receiver. "It's me, Annie. Are you decent? I'm not alone." After lis-tening for a moment, she said, "Okay. Be right up."

It occurred to Matt that he probably ought to offer to wait in the lobby or even in his car, but the words stuck in his throat, and he had to admit he wanted to know exactly who was staying with Annie.

When he and Annie walked into her tiny living room moments later, he was startled, but whether by the intensity of the relief he felt at seeing a young girl sitting cross-legged on the couch, or by the teenager herself, he wasn't sure.

Cadaverously skinny, poured into artfully tat-tered jeans, and lost somewhere inside a huge fluorescent-green T-shirt pulled in at the waist with a motorcycle belt, her short platinum hair oddly spiked and orange-streaked, she was diffi-cult not to stare at. Fortunately she didn't notice Matt's dumbfounded reaction—her eyes were glued to a television game show.

"Sorry," Annie said with a wry grin. "There's no *Gunsmoke or Green Acres* on Darlene's program lineup. Her favorite shows are *Wheel Of Fortune* and *The Price Is Right.*

As Matt smiled and glanced idly around, Annie tried not to be self-conscious about her unpreten-tious apartment. It was clean and it served her purposes, and she wasn't out to impress anyone as Dolly Decorator, she reminded herself. "Darlene Munro, this is Matt Harper," she said briskly. "He's going to wait while I pick up a few things, and then we're off. Have you heard from your brother?"

Darlene nodded and vaguely smiled, her gaze remaining fixed on the tube action. "He's coming over in about an hour to pick me up."

"Great," Annie said, then turned to Matt. "I'll only be a couple of minutes."

Nodding, he lowered himself into a comfortable but very plain, boxlike chair upholstered in a nubbed beige fabric. Institutional, he thought. Annie had rented a furnished place. Obviously she wasn't settling in. He wondered why it bothered him that she was so eager to leave Houston.

He tried to watch the game show, but he'd never liked the things, so he hadn't learned the rules. They were a maze of confusion as far as he was concerned. Besides, *M*A*S*H* was playing on another channel.

Finally a commercial broke in, and Matt tried to think of something to say to Darlene. Asking what grade she was in didn't seem like a likely icebreaker with this particular girl. A casual "Who's your hairdresser?" would be worse, so Matt searched his mind for some interesting trivia to offer about Vanna White. It was a vain quest. He didn't know anything at all about Vanna White. Now, Loretta Swit . . .

"Is Annie on a case for you?" Darlene suddenly asked, hitting the mute button on the remote control. "Are you a client of hers?"

"As a matter of fact, yes," Matt answered, though he didn't intend to be Annie's client for very long. Something else in her life, maybe. But not her client.

"She'll do a good job," Darlene said solemnly. "Annie came through for me, and I'm not even paying her. I can't. A guy ripped me off at the bus station a couple of days ago."

"Didn't you go to the police?" he asked Darlene.

"Well sure, right away. That's how I met Annie. See, the cops were, like, major useless. All they wanted to do was phone my parents and tell them to come to get me. Can you believe it? I'm from L.A., you know."

"I didn't know," Matt said politely, baffled by the conversation. The game show had been easier to follow. He wondered which episode of *M*A*S*H* was on. One of the old ones, maybe, with McLean Stevenson.

"So the desk sergeant's sitting there," Darlene continued, "and he's, like, telling me I can wait on a bench for my folks to come and get me, and I'm saying he's gotta be kidding, and Annie's there filling out a report on some case she's just solved. She comes over and talks to me, and the next thing I know I'm here."

Matt scowled, beginning to get interested—and a little concerned. "So what now? Are you going to stay here at Annie's place? What about your mom and dad?"

"Are you kidding? Annie made me call them right away. But see, I'd had a fight with them. I came to cool out for a while with my older brother. The trouble was, he'd gone out of town on, like, business, so I was kind of stuck. Anyway, he's back now and he's coming to get me. He offered to pay Annie for all she did, but she won't take anything. Did you know she tracked down the guy who grabbed my purse? In one day, can you believe it? Like, one day was all it took her to nail that sucker. He'd spent my money, but there wasn't much to start with. At least I got back all my I.D. and the purse itself, which is great, 'cause it's, like, real expensive leather." Darlene fell silent and hit the button to bring back the television sound as the commercial break ended and the game show came on again.

Annie strode back into the room moments later, a tote bag slung over one shoulder. "All set," she told Matt.

He eyed the tote bag as he got to his feet. "That's it? That's your suitcase?"

"I'm no clotheshorse, Mr. Harper." She went to Darlene, bent down, and gave the girl a quick hug. "You keep in touch, okay?"

Without missing a single spin of the fortune wheel, Darlene returned the hug. "You bet. I'll lock up on my way out, and then, like, slide the key under the door. Thanks for everything, Annie. Someday I'll pay you back."

"Just pass it on," Annie said. "You see somebody who needs a bit of help, do what you can."

Darlenge giggled. "You got it, Annie."

Impulsively, Matt reached into his breast pocket, took out a business card, and handed it to the teenager. "If, like, anything goes wrong . . ." He stopped and frowned. Was teenage talk contagious? "Anyway, my answering service number is on that card, so if you need to call Annie . . ."

"Thanks. Hey, you Texans are numero uno," Darlene said, looking away from the TV screen long enough for her approving gaze to take in both Annie and Matt.

They laughed, said another good-bye, and left.

On the way to his car, Matt didn't ask Annie why she was picking up strays and solving cases for free when she needed cash. He already knew the answer; she was a real mark. He would put down odds her soft heart was what his mother had taken aim at to talk her into this case.

She was also a nervous wreck, Matt thought as he saw her worrying at her lower lip. Maybe he ought to tell her that the situation at his place wasn't going to be quite as difficult as she thought.

No, he told himself firmly. For one thing, he wasn't sure himself how difficult it was going to be.

Soon enough they both would find out.

Five

"You call this place a *small* apartment?"

She'd wondered when she'd first stepped into Matt's penthouse hideaway why he'd furnished his living room so sparsely, with marble-tiled floors and no carpet, only a couple of straight-backed chairs, an antique white table against one wall, and an ornate mirror with a gold-leaf frame over the table.

Then she'd caught a glimpse of high-ceilinged rooms beyond a wide, arched doorway, and she'd realized she was standing in the apartment's foyer.

"Compared to my mother's condo, it *is* small," Matt said, then waited for Annie to turn on him in fury for deliberately leading her to believe she would be sharing uncomfortably close quarters with him.

Annie was considering giving Matt a black eye as she realized that he'd conned her. There she'd been, picturing a seductive bachelor lair. . . . But before she could wind up for her best shot, she spied an enormous bouquet of flowers on the table. A woman's touch, she thought with a sinking sensation.

Then she caught a whiff of something cooking. Something delicious.

A woman in the kitchen, she decided, her hands curling into fists.

"Matt, is that you, sweetie?" she heard.

A woman's voice.

Annie took a step backward and shot Matt a look. "Why didn't you—" she started to demand, but stopped abruptly as she heard approaching footsteps.

A small, plump strawberry blonde breezed into the foyer with her arms outstretched toward Matt. Reaching him, she stood on tiptoe to cradle his face between her two hands and give him an affectionate kiss. "How lovely to see you, Matthew," she said, then turned to beam at Annie. "This must be the young lady you mentioned on the phone."

"That's right, Aunt Judith. My bodyguard, Annie Brentwood."

The woman looked Annie up and down once, then laughed softly. "I see," she said in a way that suggested she definitely didn't see at all.

Annie didn't mind the derision as much as usual. She was too busy breathing a sigh of relief. Aunt Judith, she repeated silently. *Aunt* Judith.

With a smile, Matt finished the introduction. "Miss Brentwood, I'd like you to meet Judith Bannister, my father's sister and my favorite aunt."

"Your only aunt," Judith said.

Matt put his arm around her and gave her a squeeze. "You'd be my favorite even if you weren't the only one, darlin'. Thanks for coming over so promptly and on such short notice."

"Oh, it's my pleasure and you know it, dear. By the way, I threw together a little green salad to go with that chili I found bubbling in your slow cooker." Judith gave Annie a worried look. "I do hope . . ."

"Thanks," Matt cut in hastily. "Will you be having dinner with us, Aunt Judith?"

"Not this evening, dear. I have a date with Perry Shaw for dinner and the symphony."

Matt didn't allow himself to grimace as Judith chattered to Annie about how much she was looking forward to the concert, even though his aunt's news disturbed him. Hoping not to be alone with Annie at all during the evening, he'd phoned Judith as soon as he'd conceded the argument with Victoria. A chaperone had seemed like a very good idea. Now it seemed that he would have to depend on his own shaky self-control for the bulk of the evening.

Still, he realized that he couldn't expect Judith to drop all her own plans, and he was glad to see her starting to go out and enjoy life again. She'd been a virtual recluse for most of the three years since her husband had died.

The Harper women took the loss of their men desperately hard, Matt mused. His father's death had nearly meant the end of his mother as well. Matt credited the demands of the company with snapping Victoria out of a terrible depression—and the beginnings of a crew of lively grandchildren had helped.

Wondering if he was capable of such consuming passion, Matt found himself glancing at Annie with a strange, unexpected sense of longing.

He dismissed the feeling. A surge of natural lust was no reason to start getting crazy ideas.

"Where did your mind drift off to?" his aunt asked, jolting Matt from his reverie.

"Oh . . . nowhere. Would you show Miss Brent-wood to her room, Aunt Judith? I'll go check on the chili." He turned to smile politely at Annie. "I thought you might feel better with another woman on the scene," he explained.

Annie was reeling. She couldn't fathom the vulnerability and confusion he'd revealed in his expression just a moment ago. She was gripped by an insane urge to put her arms around him, sift her fingers through his silky hair, and rain soft kisses over his face. She ought to be seething at him, she told herself. She ought to wring his neck for any number of excellent reasons. Yet all she wanted to do was hold him.

Suddenly she realized that Matt's searching gaze was locked with hers, and Aunt Judith was looking on with great interest. "Who made the chili?" Annie asked, needing to break the silence.

"I did," Matt answered. "I started it before I left for the office this morning, and my slow cooker has done the rest."

"It smells wonderful," Annie murmured.

Judith frowned again. "I just hope—"

"You do know which room to take Annie to, Aunt Judith?" Matt interrupted.

The woman laughed. "I should think so, Matt." She looked around, her brows raised. "Annie, where are your suitcases?"

Annie patted the tote bag still slung over her shoulder. "This is it, Mrs. Bannister."

"My goodness, you do travel light," the woman commented. "And please call me Judith. It makes me feel so old when young people use my last name. Now, shall we go and get you settled in, Annie?"

All the Harpers seemed to prefer informality,

Annie thought as she followed Judith through the arched doorway to a hall that obviously led to the bedrooms. Except for *Mr.* Harper, with his "Miss Brentwood."

Her eyes widened when Judith opened the door to one of the guest rooms. "We've put you next to Matt, dear." The woman smiled devilishly as she added, "So you can protect him, of course."

Annie's pulse leapt into the kind of hysterical jig she was beginning to get accustomed to in situations like this. Her room was right next to Matt's. She struggled to concentrate on her surroundings, her glance taking in the classic lines of the cherrywood furniture, the soothing shades of sea green and soft gold. The room was totally unlike the sleek decor of Matt's office. Annie found herself wondering what his bedroom was like, whether it boasted the same understated, traditional elegance, whether his bed was a four-poster . . . whether he slept naked . . . She choked on a sudden intake of air.

"Are you all right?" Judith asked.

Annie nodded.

"I trust you like this room, dear?"

"I believe I can cope," Annie teased, then noticed Judith's genuine concern. "Good heavens, the place is fit for the Empress Josephine herself!" Complete with a potential Bonaparte right next door, she added silently, sinking onto a nearby slipper chair. "I'm sure I'll be extremely comfortable," she assured Judith without much conviction.

Judith smiled, obviously pleased, and waved vaguely toward a door in the far corner. "You have your own bathroom, of course. One of the beauties of this lovely big apartment is that guests can feel ever so private. He had it designed that way. The main reason he bought such a spacious place is he wanted his friends—who live all over the country—to be able to stay right here when they visit instead of going all the way out to the ranch or even, heaven forbid, taking a hotel room. Matt's so considerate."

Annie had to agree. Matt was very considerate, calling in a chaperone to make this ordeal a little easier to cope with. Of course, it would have been nice if he'd told her about his thoughtfulness, but she knew why he hadn't: He wouldn't miss a single opportunity to shake her up in the hope of shaking her loose. "Are Matt's wrangles with his mother serious?" she blurted out.

Judith laughed and shook her head. "Those two. Honestly, they're such a pair of actors. They're not just mother and son, Annie. They're best friends. They have battles because they're both strong-willed—and for the sheer fun of it."

Since Judith seemed willing to talk, Annie thought she'd clear up another of her questions. "Who's the real head of Harper Industries? Victoria or Matt?"

"Victoria *and* Matt," Judith answered. "When he turned twenty-five and took his place in the company—according to the very clearly laid-out plan in Owen's will—Matt was supposed to relieve Victoria of her temporary command. But he refused to let his mother step aside. He said he needed her experience to guide him, and perhaps he meant every word, but I happen to know he loved the way she'd blossomed during her tenure as caretaker president. He didn't think it was fair for her to have to hand over the reins to him just because Owen hadn't realized how gifted in business Victoria would turn out to be. So he got the board to agree that she should stay on as chairman while he took the title of president, which makes her the top dog, except she insisted on putting through a resolution giving Matt a final veto—which he's never exercised. It's all very complicated, but they seem to operate comfortably with their division of roles and powers. It's quite remarkable, really."

"Remarkable," Annie echoed at last, then smiled and returned to a less emotionally charged subject. "And so is this apartment. It's lovely, though First Empire isn't what I'd expected to find in a bachelor's place."

Once again, Judith looked pleased. "Actually, I did the decorating," she explained. "Matt gave me carte blanche, and I thought the Napoleonic style suited him."

"It certainly does," Annie murmured.

"I'd love to give you a tour, dear, after I've checked on your meal," Judith said eagerly as she moved to go. "That is, if you'd like one."

Annie didn't particularly want a tour. The less she saw of her client's personal life, the better. The less she had to know about the man, the better. The less contact she had with him, the better. He was too good to be true. She preferred to deal only with the love-'em-and-leave-'em Matt who would stoop to anything to make her quit her job. Aware, however, that Judith was proud of her handiwork and wanted to show it off, Annie nodded. "I'd like a tour," she said quietly.

After Judith had gone, Annie began unpacking the few things she'd brought for what she hoped would be a brief stay. She heard movements in the next room, then the sound of running water.

She groaned softly. Matt was taking a shower. Probably with that soap that smelled so wonderful. He was lathering it over his chest . . . his muscular arms—"Cut!" she whispered, as if she could end the unnerving scene with a directorial command to the rolling camera of her imagination.

It didn't work.

Apartment-tour time, she thought with sudden eagerness, going into her private bathroom to splash cold water over her face and retouch her makeup.

She was on her way to rejoin Judith before Matt had turned off his shower.

The table on the balcony glowed in the soft pink light of a hurricane candle, the silver gleamed, the china and crystal sparkled.

Annie was alone with Matt under a full moon and brightly flickering stars, sweet night air mingling with his just-showered scent, a warm breeze teasing her skin. She was trying not to think about the way he looked in jeans and a polo shirt, the soft denim hugging his taut thighs and hips, the muscles of his arms rippling with his movements, his wavy hair slightly damp.

She wished she'd changed from her business clothes and taken time for more than a quick freshening up. She felt a little wilted. Yet to have stayed in that room with Matt standing naked a wall away would have been insane.

"So you're all settled in?" Matt asked as he filled two pilsner glasses with ice-cold beer.

"Your aunt showed me around the place before she left," Annie said. "Everything's . . ." She swallowed hard as Matt smiled at her, his blue-green eyes as inviting as a Caribbean grotto and maddeningly knowing. She was certain he was aware of his effect on her and was enjoying her discomfort. "Everything's magnificent," she said without a single thought for swagged valances and Recamier chaise longues.

"Aunt Judith did a great job," Matt agreed, then felt compelled—though he had no idea why—to clarify to Annie that the apartment didn't reflect his real preferences. "To be honest, I'm more comfortable with the things we have at the ranch—standard Western style, the kind of place where you can put your feet up without feeling guilty. But I use this apartment more for entertaining than for living, so I figured it was a perfect place for my aunt to showcase her talents when she started her interior decorating career a few years ago. It worked too. She has quite a client list now."

Annie felt like screaming. How dare Matt Harper turn out to be so sweet? He probably wasn't, she told herself. There likely wasn't any Aunt Judith. He'd hired some actress to pretend to be his aunt and gush on and on about how wonderful he was. It was all part of some trick. His own mother had warned that he'd try anything.

"You're sure beer is what you'd rather have?" Matt asked as he gave Annie her tall, foaming pilsner glass. "I do have some very good wine—"

"Beer goes better with chili," she said firmly.

Matt frowned, wishing Annie weren't being such an appreciative, easy-to-please guest. She made him feel guilty. As he dished up her helping of chili from the steaming tureen, he began having second thoughts about the rotten stunt he was playing on her.

"I can hardly wait," she said with genuine enthusiasm. "I love chili."

The pallid Eastern variety, Matt thought with a stab of guilt. But he refused to give in to his reservations. What was a dirty-tricks campaign without dirty tricks? He had to get this woman off the case and out of his apartment before his libido got the best of him. His self-control had never been so sorely tested before, and he still couldn't figure out why a minx like Annie Brentwood was shaking him up so badly. "Dig in," he said with forced cheer when he'd filled his own bowl. "By the way, if you want some dried chili peppers, they're in the dish beside the salt and pepper." There wasn't much chance she'd want anything after her first taste, he mused, except a long, soothing pull of her beer.

Watching surreptitiously as Annie dipped her spoon into the deadly concoction and raised it to her lips. Matt barely restrained himself from reaching out to stop her.

Annie swallowed, frowned, waited a moment, then tried another bite and went through the same ritual.

Matt stared at her.

His expression was the giveaway to Annie, along with his tense watchfulness. She said nothing, deliberately drawing out the suspense, knowing he expected her to clutch her throat, chugalug her beer, and quit then and there out of rage or pain or both. "I think . . . ." she said at last, then paused again and smiled apologetically. "If you don't mind . . . I'd like . . . a bit more zip." She reached for the dried peppers.

Matt immediately suspected Annie knew what he'd been planning. He also suspected she was stubborn enough to suffer just to disappoint him.

His eyes widened in horror at the liberal lacing of peppers she added.

Still smiling, Annie tasted the chili again, waited, gave her head a little shake, then added another sprinkle and tried it again. Finally she nodded with satisfaction. "Now it's perfect," she said, tucking into the doctored dish with lusty enthusiasm.

"Annie, wait. I admit it," Matt said hastily. "I played a crummy trick on you. But remember, I'd cooked the chili before I met you."

"And tossed in a few extra peppers when we arrived this evening?" she asked, arching one brow.

Matt winced. "Okay, a few. But this is the way I like my food. Hot, hotter, hottest."

"There's a lot I like and admire about you Texans," Annie interrupted calmly. "But I get the biggest kick out of the general assumption that everything in this state is an *est.*"

Matt scowled. "An *est*?"

"As in big*gest,* tall*est,* sweet*est,* rich*est*—and, of course, *hottest.* It's charming. It really is. But if you think this chili is a barn-burner, you haven't tasted my Madras Meltdown."

"Your Madras Meltdown?" Matt repeated, still not sure whether Annie was putting on an incredibly brave act.

"It's the kind of curry my Great Aunt Margaret taught me to make."

Matt liked the way Annie's pronunciation of aunt was somewhere between *ant* and *awnt.* He enjoyed the defiant, upward tilt of her chin. And he much preferred the gleam of triumph in her eyes to the teary glaze his chili was supposed to have caused. There was just too much about Annie he liked. "Where did your aunt learn to make a five-alarm curry?" he asked, realizing he'd better keep the conversation going or risk exploring Annie's many charms all too closely.

"She married an Englishman, and they spent several years in India back in the forties," Annie explained, then paused to savor another mouthful of chili before going on. "Aunt Margaret not only developed a taste for the food there, she learned to prepare it herself, so when they moved to Boston she naturally served it as a special treat for dinner guests. My parents and sisters acted like martyrs. You'd have thought they'd been forced to swallow flaming swords. But as soon as I took my first bite I thought I'd died and gone to the Taj Mahal." Annie smiled. "I felt much the same way when I tried my first honest-to-goodness Texas chili."

Matt found himself ridiculously pleased that Annie shared his enthusiasm for spicy food. "Would you make one of your Madras Meltdowns for me?" he asked with a grin. "Or do you still know how?"

"Of course I do," Annie said, laughing. "I started subsisting on Third World ethnic cuisine before it got to be trendy. Indian, Indonesian, Thai. A person can eat very well without paying a sultan's ransom. My budget and I have had reason to thank Great Aunt Margaret for her cooking lessons."

"Such as when your business partner walked out on you without a thought for your crimped cash flow," Matt commented.

Annie fervently wished she'd held her tongue about her business difficulties. Quickly she asked, "What do you have to answer for?"

Matt frowned. "Aside from trying to burn a hole through your tongue—and failing—I have nothing to answer for that I can think of offhand. Any special reason for asking? Or do you just enjoy knocking me off-stride with non sequiturs?"

"You don't even recognize the phrase?" Annie said, her eyes wide with amazement. "I can't believe you, Matt Harper! Somebody writes and says you have a lot to answer for, adds a few pointed comments about how soon you'll face a highly unsympathetic grilling, and you toss aside the letter and don't give it another thought."

"Because that's how much attention that garbage deserves," Matt said evenly. "And I have no idea what's meant by the specific line you quoted. Any other questions?"

Annie helped herself to a chunk of crusty bread. "Do you know anyone who drives a pale yellow car, maybe a Bonneville or something like that?"

"Why do you ask?"

"It seemed to follow us here, starting three blocks from your office right to the last turnoff, the one onto your street. I kept seeing its reflection in the glass buildings we passed, so I started watching in the side mirror."

"Did you get the license number?"

Annie shook her head. "The car wasn't close enough."

"Then why did you think it was following us?" Matt asked, his eyes twinkling with amusement at how wholeheartedly Annie got into her detective number.

. More of his damn mockery, Annie thought.

"Because it took every turn you did along the way, and there were quite a few of them," she answered, refusing to let him get a rise out of her.

"There are a lot of apartments in this building," Matt pointed out with the measured patience of a reasonable man dealing with an overly suspicious and excitable female. "And there are three buildings in this complex. I think we're dealing with a coincidence, Miss Brentwood."

"Possibly," Annie agreed with an icy smile.

Matt was getting frustrated. He didn't want Annie to be so agreeable. He wanted to fence with her. Make her mad. Send her storming to her room—preferably locking the door behind her. "Well, I'm sorry, but I can't think of anyone who owns a car like that," he said in his most patronizing tone. "And I've never noticed it following me before. Of course, I'm not inclined to watch for that sort of thing, not being given to paranoia. And you didn't mention the car while it was supposedly on our tail, I might add."

Temper, Annie warned herself. *Don't let him get to you.* "I didn't mention it because I knew you'd laugh it off, exactly the way you're doing. But maybe you should try being a bit paranoid for a while, Mr. Harper," she said cordially. "After all, somebody *is* out to get you."

"Somebody who's thoughtful enough to warn me in advance?" Matt said, pronouncing each syllable as slowly and carefully as if he were talking to a dull-witted five-year-old. "Tell me, Miss Brentwood, why the letters of warning?"

She shrugged. "Who knows? Maybe for the pleasure of seeing you squirm. Obviously this banana-head doesn't realize that Matt Harper wouldn't allow himself to squirm if he found himself staked out in a colony of rattlesnakes."

Matt's lips twitched as he tried not to smile.

Annie was determined not to let him get her dander up. "Or maybe our stamp-licking friend is a little short on nerve and is writing the letters as a warm-up exercise. Or putting threats on paper as a sort of commitment, a declaration of intent."

"Or maybe we're simply dealing with a crank."

"It's possible," Annie agreed. "But I'm curious about something. Why do you have such tight security here? The doorman could be a stand-in for Stallone, except he doesn't look as friendly as Rambo. The elevator won't come all the way up to this floor unless you use your special key. There's a closed-circuit television camera in the hallway. And then there's your apartment itself: With all the locks and alarms here, the British crown jewels would be safe. Are you certain you don't have enemies who worry you a little?"

"I'm sure I do have enemies," Matt answered offhandedly. "But I don't waste time worrying about them. I have valuables in this apartment— Aunt Judith's taste is expensive. I occasionally have guests who like to feel protected. And Victoria, backed as usual by the tribe, insisted I had to get Charlie to rig the place a year ago, after one of our friends in the next building barely missed being a corporate-kidnapping victim."

Annie tried not to keep dwelling on the guests who liked to feel protected. Diamond-laden beauties, no doubt. "Do you do everything your mother asks?"

Matt was about to retort that Victoria had dragged out the tired but effective chestnut that he owed it to the company as well as to the family to be responsible about his personal security, but he changed his mind. His lips curved in a slow, teasing grin. "Of course I do everything she asks. Isn't it obvious I'm a mama's boy? Aren't I the stereotype of the dutiful son?"

Annie rolled her eyes at the utter nonsense he was spouting now. He was just making fun of her for asking such an obviously ridiculous question. "If you're a typical mama's boy, then boxing gloves outsell flowers on Mother's Day. Now, what enemies, specifically, can you tell me about?"

Matt took a deep breath and let it out slowly, then spoke again in measured, careful syllables. "I have no idea, my one-track-mind friend. I just assume I'm not universally popular."

"Think," Annie persisted. "Think hard."

He passed one hand over his eyes and sighed. "Okay. I'm thinking. Enemies. Let's see, apart from Victoria . . ."

Throwing down her napkin like a gauntlet, Annie pushed back her chair and got to her feet. "I'll clear up," she muttered, stacking the plates. "I don't seem to be able to accomplish anything else around here since you seem determined to make light of these threats."

Matt jumped up and rounded the table, stopping himself within an inch of hauling Annie into his arms. He ached to hold her. Physically ached, as if his whole body were suddenly aware of being incomplete. He stared down at Annie, battling the temptation to kiss her—the *need* to kiss her, the primitive drive to fuse with her. But her soft brown eyes were too startled. Her slender body was too tense. If he so much as touched her, he would feel like a leopard pouncing on a field mouse. "I'll help," he said at last.

Annie breathed for the first time since Matt had leapt out of his chair. Certain he was going to kiss her again, she'd felt her lips parting and swelling in anticipation of his mouth capturing hers. Her disappointment at his retreat appalled her. "I'd rather have your help solving this case," she told him, her voice tight.

"There is no case, Miss Brentwood," Matt snapped.

She gave him the most disdainful look she could muster. "I've changed my mind, Mr. Harper," she said coldly, putting the plates back on the table. "K.P. duty isn't in my job description. Do the damn dishes yourself."

Matt watched her march back inside the apartment and a moment later heard her bedroom door shut.

Good, he told himself. Mission accomplished.

He cleared the table and did the dishes. Then he went to his own room, put on some earphones, and tuned into the TV Golden Oldies channel in time to catch a *WKRP* episode.

Within five minutes he'd turned it off and was sitting glaring at the blank screen. When even Loni Andersen couldn't make him laugh and forget about the infuriating woman on the other side of the wall, he was in big trouble.

Six

For the next several days Annie and Matt butted heads like a couple of obstinate mountain goats, each trying to bounce the other into the next county.

Matt dragged Annie to meetings all over the state, usually flying to his destinations and piloting the plane himself. His small Cheyenne made even Victoria nervous. He wasn't entirely surprised to discover that Annie liked traveling in small planes. What was more, she didn't seem too worried about his skills—or didn't let on, if she was at all edgy. She did make him cool his heels while she checked out the aircraft right down to the fire extinguisher, just as she always did a quick once-over of his car, but Matt didn't mind. The anonymous letters were coming thick and fast, and he was starting to take them more seriously.

He tried another ploy to shake Annie up a little. During business conferences, he put her on the spot several times, asking her questions, daring her to reply without making a fool of herself or blowing her cover. He was prepared each time to rescue her—if only to stay in control of the merger negotiations—but she didn't need his help. To his secret enjoyment, she was either knowledgeable enough to come up with a valid response, or she was able to bluff her way through.

As if the days weren't charged with enough temptation, Matt found the evenings at his apartment a constant blend of torment and delight. His desire for Annie was increasingly difficult to control, shoring up his determination to push her into quitting. Yet her effervescent personality made him want to keep her around indefinitely. She was fun to be with, always bubbling with comical tales of her adventures as a private eye. Aunt Judith doted on her, and Matt found himself musing about how bland his life had been before Annie had breezed into it.

But during the course of those evenings he learned something vital about Annie: Unlike her ex-partner, she honored her commitments. Whether she was facing a baseball bat in the hands of a "knuckle-walking deadbeat" whose car she'd been sent to repossess, or risking a bent nose from a slammed door when she was serving a summons, the bottom line was that Annie got the job done.

And this woman, Matt thought with a private laugh at himself, was supposed to resign in a snit, even though she'd given her word to Victoria that she wouldn't? He was beginning to understand just what he was up against.

Friday morning arrived. Annie was still Matt's bodyguard-decoy-investigator, and he was more resolved than ever to move her from the professional to the strictly personal area of his life.

He poked his head through her open office door. "Do you own jeans?"

"Of course," Annie said, not even glancing up from her computer screen. She'd found it wise to look at Matt as little as possible. His sensual impact on her, instead of waning, was intensifying. She peered intently at the screen for a moment, then hit a series of keys. "Why would you want to know if I own jeans?"

"Because we're leaving for the Lazy H after lunch."

Annie smiled. During her entire year in Texas, she'd never been to a ranch. "I'll have to go to my place for the jeans," she said, then picked up a pencil and jotted down a note from the information on her screen. "Any special reason for the trip?"

"I spend most weekends there. So does Victoria," Matt answered. He didn't add that Aunt Judith had her own plans for the next couple of days and couldn't chaperone them, or that the thought of being alone with Annie in his apartment would put too much strain on his overtaxed scruples.

Strange, he thought as his gaze devoured her, how had Annie gotten under his skin. It certainly wasn't because she tried. She seemed unaware of her feminine potential. Even her sense of style appeared to center on her ability to keep rotating the components of two outfits and a few extras. "You don't waste much time fussing about clothes, do you," he blurted out.

Annie looked up for an instant, then hastily returned her attention to her work. "Is there something wrong with my clothes?" she asked airily.

"Not at all!" Matt said, feeling a flush rise up from his neck. "They're very . . . attractive. It's just that . . . you don't seem to have a . . . well, an extensive wardrobe."

"I don't need an extensive wardrobe," she said, trying to sound unconcerned. "I'm dressed suitably, am I not?"

"Of course! I didn't mean to suggest otherwise. You look great!" He cursed himself under his breath. Now she was reducing him to a stammering oaf. "I guess it's just that I'm accustomed to women who love to buy clothes."

Annie forced herself to look at him, summoning her most withering peer-down-the-nose hauteur. "Mr. Harper, I am a Boston Brentwood. We do not *buy* our clothes. We *have* our clothes." With a sniff she'd learned at her grandmother's aristocratic knee, she returned her gaze to her computer terminal.

Matt blinked, stared at her, then burst out laughing as he realized he'd just been put in his place by a genuine blueblood. "Handed down through generations, are they?"

Annie chose not to answer. She saw no reason to admit she'd bought her two sets of washable, no-iron coordinates at a Saks sale a year ago. "Exactly where *is* the Lazy H, anyway?" she asked instead.

"About a hundred miles west of here," Matt answered. "What are you checking there?"

"Employee records."

"For what?"

"I'm making note of changes. People who've been hired in the last six months, people who've left."

"Why?"

"I'm just doing my job, Mr. Harper. Investigation is research. Often boring research that leads nowhere. But it's necessary. Are we flying to the ranch?"

"Driving."

Annie's pulse quickened. Since moving to Texas, she'd been so busy working, she hadn't seen the countryside until recently, and then only from Matt's plane. And her heart always missed a few beats at the prospect of traveling with him. "I can scoot home right now to pick up a few things," she suggested.

"No need," Matt commented. "We'll stop off at your place on our way out of town."

"Whatever you say, boss," Annie murmured.

Matt frowned and returned to his office. Except for that single moment when she'd delivered her regal rebuke, she hadn't looked at him once. Hadn't spared him a glance.

Her indifference was driving him crazy.

Annie was uncommonly contented during the journey to the ranch, her deep-seated tensions ebbing with the passing of each mile. "How big is the Lazy H?" she asked Matt after they'd been quiet for some time.

He was startled from a trancelike state. He wasn't sure what he'd expected of the drive with Annie, except perhaps an awkward, tense silence in which they both tried to pretend there were no sparks flying between them. But so far, despite definite silences and undeniable sparks, the atmosphere had been companionable. "Sorry," he said with a smile. "What did you say?"

Annie wondered what he'd been thinking about

so hard. Probably some new plot to get her dander up, she decided. "I asked how big your ranch is."

"Oh, I'd say it's about half an RI," Matt answered, his eyes twinkling.

Annie searched her memory banks for several moments, but finally had to give up. "What's an RI?"

Matt gave her a crooked grin. "A Rhode Island. Here in Texas we have our own scale of measurements."

"I keep forgetting," Annie said with a grin. "Texas bragging is no myth."

Matt needed no further encouragement to indulge in some *real* Texas bragging, enthusing over the unique wonders of his home state, going on at length about its incredible variety. He pointed out a wide, lazy, emerald river and said that all Texas rivers were the widest and prettiest and laziest to be found anywhere, just as Texas blue bonnets were the bluest of flowers, Texas skies the brightest, Texas air the sweetest.

They both laughed when Annie pointed out how little time it had taken him to lapse into the *est* descriptions she'd teased him about. She wondered if he'd done it on purpose. "It's strange, though," she murmured. "Even after a year in Houston my mental image of the state is like an old sepia photograph, all flat and beige."

"Then you have to experience a sunset at the ranch," Matt said. "Better still, a sunrise."

Annie wondered if she'd been a little too hasty in deciding to head back East as soon as her lease ran out. After choosing to move to a place that would be completely different from New England, she'd experienced a sort of culture shock; Texas had seemed all *too* different from anything she'd known before. She hadn't really given it a chance.

Matt was up at the first glimmer of light on Saturday morning, heading for the stables to saddle his favorite stallion for a long, solitary ride.

To his surprise, Annie was there ahead of him.

Matt swallowed hard as his glance took in her nicely fitted jeans and the gentle curve of her breasts under a denim jacket and a red cashmere pullover that had seen better days. "What are you doing here?" he asked, deciding he'd never seen anything as appealing as Annie Brentwood in a black Hi-Roller, a specialty hat like the kind card sharps once wore. Trust her to go for that style, he mused.

Annie leapt in startled excitement. "Oh! I didn't know you . . . I didn't realize . . . Victoria told me it would be all right if I rode White Star." She looked at the horse she'd been saddling. "This *is* White Star, I hope? I mean, judging by her markings . . ."

"That's right," Matt said, taking off his Stetson and raking his fingers through his hair. "So I can't even hit the old lonesome trail without my bodyguard?"

"I didn't know you were planning to ride this morning," Annie protested. "I thought you were still in bed. Yesterday you said I should see a sunrise, and last night when Victoria arrived I asked her permission to use one of the horses. She said I could take this mare, so that's what I'm doing. Or was doing. Now I'm not sure. I don't want to suffocate you, but on the other hand . . ."

Matt suppressed a grin at the thought of putting Annie through a few paces on horseback. "I suppose I could be riding into an ambush. Maybe you'd better come along. At the very least you could ride for help."

"You don't mind?" Annie asked, ignoring his irony.

Matt's glance flickered over her with a detachment that totally belied what he was feeling. "Where'd you get the hat?"

"Victoria," Annie answered. "It belongs to one of your sisters."

"Looks good on you," Matt said, keeping the turmoil of his emotions well hidden. "Have you ever ridden before, or do you just figure you can hop aboard and go?"

"I'll manage," she said curtly. "I seem to have done all right so far. This mare didn't saddle herself."

Matt shrugged, realizing she had a point. As usual when Annie was around, he wasn't thinking too clearly. He wondered when she'd learned to saddle a horse—and why. But he chose not to ask. "Let's go, then," he said at last. "I can put up with you if you can *keep* up with me."

Within a very few minutes, he was smiling with grudging admiration. Keep up? Annie looked as if she'd been born on a saddle. "Okay," he said in resignation after half an hour on the trail. Was there anything this woman couldn't do? "Where did you learn to handle a horse that way? Or is it that Boston Brentwoods don't *learn* to ride, they simply *ride*?"

Annie laughed happily. She couldn't remember when she'd ever been so exhilarated. The sunrise was a breathtaking display of brilliantly colored ribbons appearing above the horizon, the air was bracing, the mare was beautifully responsive.

And Matt, she thought as she forgot her taboo against staring at him. Matt was magnificent. With his tanned skin, sun-streaked hair, and blue-green eyes, he was like part of the spectacular landscape while dominating it with his special vibrance. He was a wonderful rider, too, controlling his spirited stallion, yet moving in such perfect harmony with the animal, he was like an extension of it. As rugged as the land itself, he was big and powerful and totally male.

"Aren't you going to answer me?" he asked, barely resisting the urge to respond to the desire in Annie's eyes by dragging her from her mare to his own mount and taking her the way she looked as if she wanted to be taken.

Annie bit down on her lower lip and tightened her grip on her reins. "I took lessons," she answered belatedly. "My parents considered riding an essential part of a young lady's education. It was the only part I liked, and the only part I was good at. Still, I managed to make them disapprove of me by preferring Western to English."

"It sounds as if you worked at making your parents disapprove of you," Matt commented idly, most of his attention and energy focused on quelling the primitive instincts Annie had aroused.

"I didn't have to work at it," Annie retorted. "I had a natural flair for bugging my folks. Same as the talent I seem to have for irritating you."

If only she knew, Matt thought, but didn't set her straight. When they were alone this way, it was more prudent to let her believe she got on his nerves.

They were quiet again for a long while. Then

Annie saw a large herd of cattle in the distance and her annoyance was driven out by curiosity. "Are those yours?" she asked.

Matt nodded.

"Longhorns?"

"That's right," Matt said. "You're full of surprises, Miss Brentwood. What do you know about Texas longhorns?"

"Just that they're regaining popularity. Low-cal cattle, I think I read somewhere. Lean meat, an asset instead of a liability in these fat-conscious days. Also known for longevity, resistance to disease, and high calf yield. And I don't know why you should be impressed that I recognized the breed." Annie smiled sweetly. "Longhorns do seem to have long horns, Mr. Harper. Even an Easterner can see that. Who runs the ranch when you're not around?"

"We have first-rate hands, and a foreman named Joe Bob Vickers who's been with us since I was a kid," Matt answered, suppressing a chuckle. Lord, how he loved Annie's feistiness! "Joe Bob's gone to Dallas for the weekend, but if you're still on the job next week, you'll meet him."

"*If* I'm still on the job?"

Matt smiled. "*If*, Miss Brentwood. You're trying to solve this case as well as protect me, aren't you? I seem to have more confidence than you that you'll track down my number one fan in no time."

Annie was furious with herself. She'd become so wary of everything Matt Harper said and did, she'd walked right into his trap. But what really bothered her was that she wasn't sure she could solve the mystery in the next week. After five days she hadn't come up with a single solid lead. "Could we ride a little faster?" she asked abruptly.

Matt nodded and broke into a canter, smiling to himself as he watched Annie. As a youngster, he'd gone with his father for these sunrise outings, and since his dad's death he'd carried on the tradition alone, fiercely guarding his solitude. The thought that he'd allow any woman to tag along wouldn't have seemed possible to him even a week ago. But having Annie with him was different. She—

Matt put up a mental stop sign. Annie was just another female, he told himself. He didn't want to dwell on the insane feeling that she was something more, that his constant urge to make love to her went beyond a physical need. He didn't care for the potentially life-altering notions she inspired in his imagination.

All at once he heard Annie's mare give a startled whinny. Turning, he saw the horse rear up, then bolt forward in a panicky gallop. Matt was struck with sick fear . . . mind-numbing cold terror. He was barely aware of taking off after Annie, of his stallion's sudden burst of speed, of catching up and grabbing White Star's reins. The blood was pounding in his head as he brought the mare to a stop and wrapped his arm around Annie's slender waist to drag her to his own saddle as if it were the only way he could be sure she was safe.

"I had her under control!" Annie protested.

Matt didn't answer. He just held Annie against his chest, barely noticing he'd knocked her hat to the ground, and buried his face in her dark hair. He was too shocked by the violence of his emotions to speak.

Annie had known the strength of Matt's arms

before, the warmth of his body, the hardness of him against her, but nothing had prepared her for what she was feeling now. His raw power, no longer in check, stunned her. Yet she kept trying to battle the feelings washing over her. "Something spooked the mare," she said, managing not to sound too shaky. "A rattler, I think. I was letting her run out her panic for a minute, that's all."

Matt gave a thick, husky laugh. "Okay, so you had her under control, and I guess I've seen too many Gene Autry reruns. But I had no way of knowing you could handle the situation." Realizing Annie's trembling body belied her brave words, he raised his head to smile at her. "You scared the hell out of me, sweetheart."

Annie gazed up at him. *Sweetheart?* And was he holding her so tightly only because he was a protective male who still wasn't quite sure she was all right? Was his heart pounding erratically because of the chase? And the expression in his eyes . . . the sudden heat emanating from him. . . . She was mesmerized as Matt slowly bent his head and touched his mouth to hers. All at once she was groaning softly, parting her lips, inviting the possessive thrusts of his tongue, craving kisses that were bruising in their intensity. Her body exploded into flames as Matt began touching her, stroking her hair, her cheeks, her shoulders and the sides of her breasts. She twined her arms around his neck and eagerly pressed herself to him as she felt his throbbing hardness against her thigh. She was incapable of rational thought. Of any thought. She could only feel and respond.

Matt vaguely knew he was doing something totally against his principles, but principles didn't seem important anymore. Nothing seemed important except that Annie was in his arms, safe and sweet and eager. Nothing counted but to kiss and caress her. Nothing mattered but the discovery that her hunger was as acute as his, her kisses as demanding as his, her body as hot with need and excitement. "Annie," he whispered as he gently pushed her away a few inches so he could slide his hand under her sweater. She was braless. Stroking her breasts, he marveled at how soft yet firm she was, how perfectly she filled his hand, how velvety and swollen her nipples were.

Dimly remembering that just a little while earlier he'd been picturing almost exactly what he was doing, Matt half-considered stripping away every bit of Annie's clothing and taking her right then and there. His imagination ran wild with the thought of turning her to face him, cupping his hands under her to make her straddle him, filling her until they both knew she belonged to him. He was crazy with wanting her that way. His depth of feeling for her was crazy. He'd met her a week before. Yet nothing seemed or felt crazy, except perhaps the losing battle against a force that was too strong to resist.

Matt's hand went to the fastening of her jeans, and Annie offered no protest. She shuddered as he slowly lowered the zipper, but when he hesitated, she tightened her arms around him and nipped at his lower lip, then stroked it with her tongue. He touched the smooth flatness of her belly and her body leapt in response. "Annie, I'm going to love you," he murmured. "It has to happen."

Annie heard his words and wondered if he were issuing a warning she was supposed to heed. But she couldn't heed it. She ached for Matt to love her, if only physically and if only for the moment.

Matt's fingers were plunging downward, gently touching the throbbing center of Annie's need, when reality intruded with a familiar buzzing sound he realized he should have been expecting. Cursing softly, he drew back his hand, then wrapped his arms around Annie and just held her. "Modern cowboys, baby," he murmured. "There's a helicopter coming, a couple of the boys checking the herd. I don't know where the hell my head is, not to have remembered about their coming by."

All at once Annie felt as if her whole body were consumed by fires of frustrated desire—and utter humiliation. As she looked up and saw the fast-approaching chopper, shame washed over her. Matt had to have known the helicopter would be coming. This interruption was no accident. She began struggling to extricate herself from his arms. "Let me go!" she cried when he kept her imprisoned against him. "Damn you, let go of me! You win, Mr. Harper. I'll tell Victoria you finally got me to say uncle, so you've achieved your purpose. Can't you at least let me salvage what little pride I have left?"

Shocked by her words and hating himself for losing control—or, he conceded more honestly, for losing it at such an inopportune moment in such a wide-open space—Matt released Annie, letting her scramble down from his horse. Picking up her hat and hastily refastening her jeans, she hurried over to White Star. The mare, grazing contentedly, looked almost amused at the trouble she'd started. It was the first time in Matt's life he'd ever felt like throttling a horse.

The copter reached them and the flying cowboys inside waved just as Annie swung up into her saddle and turned back toward the ranch, then gave a quick dig of her sneakers into the mare's flanks and took off at a gallop.

Matt halfheartedly returned the cheerful greeting before following Annie at just enough distance to keep an eye on her in the unlikely event of another mishap. He wanted to catch up with the woman, to make her understand that he hadn't staged what had happened. Yet he knew he'd be wiser to do with Annie what she'd planned to do with White Star—let her run off her panic. He stayed back.

By the time they reached the ranch, Matt realized the extent of the mess he'd gotten himself into. He'd been given a clear glimpse of Annie's simmering sensuality. He'd had a taste of what the two of them could share. And he'd started falling for the woman. Hard. But thanks to his stupid declaration of war and his adolescent dirty-tricks campaign to get her to quit the case, he wouldn't give a nickel for his chances of making her believe his feelings were real.

What he could do, however, was talk to Victoria. With any luck, he might get to her before Annie did. Maybe his mother would see at last why the situation was impossible. Perhaps she would let Annie off the hook and even put in a good word for him.

His spirits rose when he managed to corner Victoria an hour later, while Annie was in her room changing her clothes. But after a brief chat with his mother, Matt's hopes plummeted again. Victoria wasn't going to be any help to him at all.

After a late lunch on Sunday, Matt ambled down to the corral to talk with a couple of the hands. Annie and Victoria lingered over coffee, sitting at the white and yellow umbrella table on the patio outside the sprawling ranch house.

Annie was quiet, wondering how to make Victoria listen to her once and for all and release her from her promise to stay on the case. Her admission the previous afternoon that she'd gotten emotionally involved with Matt hadn't cut any ice whatsoever with the woman. "Well, dear," Victoria had said with an understanding smile as she'd reached across the kitchen table to pat Annie's hand, "in my opinion you're that much more valuable to me. I'd hate to have some cold fish looking after my son's welfare. And what's so terrible about a little emotional involvement, anyway? Matthew's still a gentleman, even if he did forget himself for a moment. Honestly, you youngsters take things much too seriously. Sorry, Annie. If you want me to let you go, you're doomed to disappointment."

Annie had managed to avoid being alone with Matt since the ill-fated dawn ride. As she watched him rest one booted foot on the corral fence and lift his hat for a moment to smooth back his unruly autumn-gold hair, she felt a resurgence of desire that just wouldn't be quelled. She couldn't imagine how she was going to cope with the situation when they returned to Houston.

"You seem to like the Lazy H," Victoria commented.

Annie put down her cup and managed a smile. She did like the Lazy H. It was a beautiful ranch in magnificent country. "Who wouldn't like it?" she murmured.

"You'd be surprised, Annie. For me, of course, it's a haven. And Matthew seems to need to come back here whenever he can to recharge his batteries. He carries a heavy load of responsibility, you know. We're an old-fashioned family in many ways, and he's the patriarch, or at least sees himself in that role. I think that's why he's always steered clear of serious involvements with young women; he already has enough females to worry about."

"But you're hardly a clinging vine, and your daughters seem to have their own lives well established," Annie couldn't help commenting.

"I know, but Harper Industries wouldn't exist without Matthew. He's the driving force. The girls were never interested, possibly because their father tried to get them to be interested, or perhaps simply because they're too much like Owen to follow in his footsteps. They had to carve out their own paths. So does Matthew, but within the framework of the company. He's the linchpin of the family, even though he's the youngest. I guess it's his attitude. His protectiveness. When he was eight he got into a scrap with a twelve-year-old smart aleck who'd taken to yelling obscenities at Mirella on the playground at school. Matthew came out of the fray sporting a black eye, but he'd sent the bigger boy home with a bloody nose. And Mirella didn't have to worry about any more obscenities. Times haven't changed. Matt's still the guardian of the entire clan."

"Victoria," Annie said slowly, "it's obvious that

to Matt I'm just another responsibility, not an effective security guard. I can't fathom why you hired me and why you insist on keeping me on the case."

Victoria sighed deeply. "It's so simple, Annie. I believe you'll find out who has a hate on for my son."

Annie shook her head. "I haven't been doing so well on that score. And really, even apart from the personal difficulties I'm having with this case, the money is bothering me. It's very nice to be raking it in, but I feel so guilty. I'm not accomplishing enough, and you're paying me to sit around in a beautiful apartment chatting with Aunt Judith and developing a silly crush—" She stopped. Victoria knew the rest and didn't seem to care. "I think we should at least renegotiate the terms."

"Don't be ridiculous," Victoria said with a low chuckle. "Heavens, considering what that mule-headed young man keeps putting you through, I probably ought to double your fee. Combat pay. How is your investigation going, though? Are you finding any likely suspects at all?"

"Not among the business colleagues I've met or researched. Matt deals too fairly with people to make them hate him. Even in merger negotia-tions he doesn't go for the jugular. How can I come up with possible enemies for a man who's so . . . so terminally *decent*?"

Victoria's lips twitched. "He's really impossible, isn't he? How about the women in his life? Have you talked to any of them?"

"He won't give me names."

"Really?" Victoria asked, arching a brow. "How interesting." She looked toward the corral and stared at Matt for several long moments. "How very interesting."

"Not that I need names from him," Annie said hastily. "I could dig up the information easily enough. And to some extent—through clippings and such—I've done a fair amount of checking. My impression is that your son is as straight and open with the ladies he goes out with as he is in business deals. He's not likely to inspire hatred there, either. But he obviously doesn't want me prying into that area of his life, so I respect his wishes."

"Why?" Victoria asked pointedly.

Annie scowled. "Because he's a client, not a criminal under investigation. I have no right to poke my nose in where it's not wanted."

"I see," Victoria said. She gazed as long and thoughtfully at Annie as she had at Matt. "You're sure you have no other reason?"

Annie looked away. She wanted to believe that her respect for her client's privacy was why she was avoiding talking to the women he dated. But she wasn't sure. And it was time, she told herself, to deal with her doubt. To *be* sure—or to get off the case, even if it meant breaking her promise to Victoria. If she couldn't do the job, she'd better find someone else to handle it.

Seven

By the middle of the week after her visit to the Lazy H, Annie was seriously considering the possibility of admitting defeat, both as a detective and as a woman of her word. The hate leters were still arriving for Matt, she wasn't getting any closer to finding out who was sending them, and she knew her feelings were getting in her way.

She was having trouble concentrating. She wasn't sleeping well. When she did sleep, she dreamed about Matt. She wished he would do something that would turn her off, such as living up to the honeybee image his mother had given him. But he seemed content to stay home in the evenings and watch his beloved Golden Oldies TV channel, or just read. And he was being *so* gentlemanly. Even when Aunt Judith went out for the evening, Matt was the soul of propriety. It was as if the searing moments on the trail at the Lazy H had never happened.

She was puzzled. It seemed logical that Matt would either pour on the sensual pressure to make her quit, or go the other way and take out some cheerleader for a bit of dining and dancing, requiring his bodyguard to tag along and watch him in action. He didn't do either. But he didn't try to help her track down his nemesis, and the long evenings at the apartment were too tense to bear.

As she rode with Matt to the office on Thursday morning, Annie renewed her private vow to step up her efforts, in the hope of tiring out her mind and her libido and solving the mystery at the same time. Find the culprit, she kept telling herself. Stamp CASE CLOSED on the Harper file. Get back to some semblance of sanity.

Unfortunately, only one lead had presented itself so far, and it wasn't very promising. Annie had managed to establish an easy camaraderie with the people at the office, hoping idle gossip might shake loose a stray clue. In the middle of a casual conversation with an accounting department manager the day before, she'd glanced up just in time to be startled by the venomous glare of an attractive brunette clerk at a nearby desk.

The woman had blinked when she'd seen Annie looking at her, then smiled as if to suggest that her mind had been on some problem, that her look of apparent hatred hadn't been aimed at anyone in particular.

Elizabeth Reynolds, Annie had noted from the nameplate on the clerk's desk. After returning to her office a few minutes later, Annie had looked at the employee files. Elizabeth Reynolds had started working for Harper Industries just six months before and had changed her home address three months later. Her immediate superior had scrawled a memo to the effect that Elizabeth had been chalking up quite a bit of absenteeism and lateness recently. *Personal problems?* the supervisor had written. *Perhaps a heart-to-heart talk?*

Then Annie had checked the parking lot lists, but the car registered for Elizabeth Reynolds was a gray Topaz, not a yellow Bonneville.

Annie sighed heavily as she watched Matt negotiating the heavy morning traffic. The Reynolds lead didn't seem worth discussing with him. He would laugh it off anyway, just as he'd continued to laugh off her insistence that a yellow Bonneville *had* followed them on several occasions, always at a careful distance and in traffic.

Matt vaguely noticed Annie's sigh, but he was dwelling on his own troubled thoughts and on a compelling urge to stop battling Annie, ask for a truce, and say he was sorry for . . . for a lot of things. Yet he couldn't. Even if he was willing to concede that his mother and the rest of the board had a right to insist on his protection, he couldn't get past two solid roadblocks where Annie was concerned: Hiding behind a woman wasn't his idea of being a man, and climbing all over a woman who worked for him wasn't his idea of being a gentleman.

Yet that very morning, when Annie had joined him for breakfast wearing her khaki skirt/ivory shell/black jacket combo, her sable hair smooth and glossy, her eyes heavy-lidded as if she'd had her own problems sleeping, he'd been within a breath of tossing aside his scruples, throwing her over his shoulder, and carrying her to his room for a three-day lovemaking marathon.

He'd managed to contain himself. Barely.

Despite the misguided but general opinion that he took his pleasures where he found them, Matt considered himself a cautious, conservative, discriminating male who had too much self-control to hop into a woman's bed against his better judgment. Yet his self-control and better judgment abandoned him when Annie was around.

No, he decided. He would *not* apologize for trying to make her quit a job she'd had no business accepting, a job that could get her hurt one way or another. He would stick to his guns. Period.

He heard Annie heave another sigh and saw her fingers creep up to massage her temple, her eyes closed.

"Headache?" he asked, reminding himself not to apologize.

Annie gave a little start, then nodded. "Just a bit."

Matt said nothing for the next few blocks. "I'm sorry," he muttered as he pulled up to a red light.

Annie snapped her head around to stare at him. "What did you say?"

He cursed silently, but gave in to the inevitable. "I'm sorry," he repeated, staring straight ahead. "I've been acting like a first-class heel. But I . . . I'm concerned about you."

"You have things backward, Mr. Harper," Annie said, hating the warmth that was coursing through her. "It's my job to be concerned about you." Irrationally, she got angry at Matt for the way he made her feel. She told herself he probably worked at being devastating, spending ages in front of the mirror to get his tawny hair rumpled just so, and no doubt countless fitting sessions at his tailor to achieve his dark blue suit's perfect taper, from his wide shoulders to his lean waist and hips.

The traffic light turned green, and Matt fell silent again, as if he had to concentrate on his driving. But he was thinking. Annie brought out his most primitive instincts. She liked to believe she was tough, but he knew better. She was made to be cherished, to be guarded from a harsh world that would take advantage of her innate gentleness. What was she doing in the private investigation business? "I can't change the way I'm built," he stated flatly.

Annie knew what he meant, but his comment sent her mind off on another erotic tangent. She didn't want to change the way Matt was built. Not in any sense. Familiar images mercilessly assailed her, though she tried not to envision smoothing her palms over every inch of his muscular body, touching her tongue to his warm, spicy skin, letting her fingers romp through the chest hair she glimpsed whenever he was dressed casually. She hoped Matt had no idea how her mouth ached for his, how the tips of her breasts hardened at the thought of being crushed against him, how a tingling heaviness had settled permanently between her thighs . . .

Audibly gasping, Annie could only hope the traffic would keep Matt's attention away from her.

But he was drawing to a stop at another red light, and he turned to look at her with a curious intentness, as if aware of her every intimate, forbidden secret.

"You don't have much staff turnover," she said, grasping for an innocuous subject. She looked out her window, hoping to hide the flush spreading over her skin.

Matt smiled quizzically. He'd have sworn, when he'd seen the expression on Annie's face, that she hadn't been thinking about staff turnover. "We're lucky that way."

"Do you have any idea why you inspire so much loyalty and continuity?" Annie asked, hoping her voice wasn't really as squeaky as it sounded to her ears.

Matt gave in to the temptation to subject Annie to a long, lazy scrutiny before starting up the car again. "You should be able to answer that one, Miss Brentwood," he drawled. "Look at the loyalty I've gotten from you."

"I wonder when I'm going to learn," she murmured.

"Learn what, Miss Brentwood? To give up?"

She faced him with her coolest smile. "No. To stop walking into verbal shootouts with a quick-draw artist who usually gets the drop on me."

Matt grinned. He'd just realized how subdued Annie had been for the last few days—and how he'd missed her buoyant chatter. She made him laugh. She made him think. She made him happy.

But he still had to make her quit.

Annie sat behind her desk, her forehead resting on the heel of her hand, her fingers splayed through her hair. "What do mean, there's nobody?" she said into the phone. "Charlie, where *is* everyone? I thought Rick Wallace was supposed to be available by now. He's good. Victoria would like him. Matt would trust him. Rick's perfect. Get him, *please*!"

"Sweetie, what do you want from me?" Charlie Dunhill demanded. "I was sure Rick would be available by today, but it hasn't worked out. And the only other person I'd trust with my biggest client is you."

"That's very nice," Annie grumbled. "I'm glad you have faith in me. But your client doesn't share your opinion of my abilities. Matt Harper wants me off the case. He's a reasonably enlightened male, but he draws the line at having me for a bodyguard."

"Well, he's wrong," Charlie answered. "You know it and I know it. Besides, Victoria wants you on the case, and she's still chief of operations over there. Does she know you've called me?"

Annie frowned, feeling guilty. But she felt guilty no matter what she did, so she forged ahead. "No, I haven't told Victoria yet, but I will if you say you'll send Rick to replace me. I'll pave the way for him, I promise. Charlie, you've got to cut me loose. At least get me somebody for the night shifts. I . . . I'm burning out."

"Look, kid, just hang in for another day or so, okay? Rick will be freed up soon."

"But Charlie—"

"Sorry, Annie. Gotta go. My favorite nurse is here to soothe my fevered brow."

As the line went dead, Annie stared at the phone in utter consternation. "Charlie," she muttered. "I oughta break your *other* leg!"

She waded back into the daunting chore of going through the staff files, concentrating this time on work histories. If someone had been with the company for a while and seemed to have been passed over for promotion, she wrote down the name and pertinent data.

But she soon found a picture emerging of a management that showed honest concern for its people. Those who didn't earn promotions often moved to different departments, sometimes several times, until they found the right niche and career progress finally began. Terrific benefits—

Harper Industries seemed genuinely committed to nurturing a productive and happy work force.

All very wonderful, Annie thought. But it didn't point to a hate-mail suspect. And as her interpretation of the files showed her how caring the Harpers were, she couldn't help scowling, her lip jutting out in an absentminded pout as she tapped the eraser end of her pencil against it. Matt treated his employees like family, and she was apparently the long-lost relative he wished had stayed lost.

"Careful," she heard. "Somebody might come along and take a nibble."

Her head snapped up and she glared at Matt. "Take a nibble of what?" she demanded, assuming he was going to tsk-tsk her about chewing her pencil. She wished he wouldn't creep up on her all the time. It was unnerving.

Matt had decided he was justified in bending his rule about getting involved with employees. After all, Annie wasn't really an employee. She was more of a . . . a colleague. She worked for herself, not for him. His definitions had been too strict.

He loped jauntily over to her desk, leaned across it, and brushed his index finger over her full lower lip. "A nibble of you," he teased.

Catching her breath, Annie reflexively bit down on the lip, narrowly missing his finger.

Matt pulled his hand back, laughed, and reached out again, this time to brush back a strand of hair that had fallen over her forehead. "How're you doin', Gumshoe? Any more clues yet?"

Annie struggled to maintain a distant attitude, though it was difficult when Matt's eyes were twinkling with fun and he was being so friendly—

and when his casual touch had made her mouth start tingling again, yearning for his kiss. "I have a number of notes to go over with you or Victoria," she said carefully. "But I think I'm wandering down a blind alley here. Very soon, Mr. Harper, you're going to have to talk to me about the . . . the ladies in your life."

"We'll look at your notes over lunch," Matt answered. He ignored the rest of what Annie had said. There was no way he was going to give her a report on the women he saw socially—or rather, the ones he'd seen before Annie had shattered his routines. "Let's go, Miss Brentwood," he said without further preamble.

It was noon and Annie realized she was hungry, but Matt's command rankled her. She longed to rebel. Aware, however, that he was trying to nudge her into doing just that, she smiled agreeably, pushed back her chair, and gathered up her notes.

Lunch, Annie discovered to her surprise, was to be a picnic in a nearby park. Matt had ordered a gourmet basket from his favorite restaurant; it was waiting for them at the reception desk in the lobby. Tina's grin as she handed the wicker basket to Matt was devilish. "Have fun, you two," she drawled.

Annie smiled vaguely at the woman, puzzled. Matt had gone to an awful lot of trouble just to win some incomprehensible victory in his Banish Brentwood campaign.

"We can walk to the park," he told her.

"Sounds great," Annie answered, annoyed to find her spirits taking flight. "What are we having? Jalapeños on rye?"

Matt chuckled. "You've already passed the spicy-food test. And you still owe me a Madras Meltdown."

"I could make one for you tonight if you like," Annie answered, deciding to confess that he'd won, that she was trying to get herself replaced. "I spoke to Charlie about getting someone else to be your bodyguard, but the person we hoped would be free isn't. So I'm afraid you're still stuck with me."

"I know. Charlie phoned me."

Annie stopped in her tracks and stared at Matt. It was a good thing she'd confessed, she thought.

Matt paused and smiled down at her. "Charlie gave me quite an earful about you, Annie."

"Namely?" she asked with a wary glance as they started walking again.

"One of the things he told me was that he would hire you full-time in a minute if you weren't so determined to stay a freelancer."

"Now I'm sorry I yelled at him," Annie remarked. "I'd better take him some brownies; Charlie loves brownies."

"Charlies also said," Matt added quietly, "that Annie Brentwood is building such a top-flight reputation in this town, even her partner's buy-out demands wouldn't have put the squeeze on her cash flow if she would quit doing freebies, like tracking down some abandoned wife's hus-band and getting him to come up with alimony, or finding a runaway teenager, or—"

"People in every profession do freebies," Annie said defensively, though she knew she wasn't a very good businessperson. That part of the opera-tion was to have been Cheryl's department. "Coun-try performers do concerts for Farm Aid, actors march for the environment, rock stars sing for someone else's supper. I'm just . . . just . . ."

"A soft-boiled detective?" Matt supplied with a grin.

Annie couldn't help laughing. "Okay. But read any detective story. Watch any movie or television show about private eyes. Try to figure out how those guys live. Haven't you noticed that they almost never take money? I've told Victoria that I feel guilty about what she's paying me, especially when I haven't come up with anything yet. Maybe you were right not to want to hire me. Maybe—"

"Another thing Charlie said," Matt cut in, "was that there are other freelancers around, but no one available who can be trusted the way you can to get to the bottom of any puzzle as fast as possible. Charlie gave you quite a buildup, Annie. A big vote of confidence."

Annie's pulse accelerated. Was Matt really being nice to her, or was he setting her up for another fall?

"Unfortunately," Matt went on, "Charlie doesn't understand my problem."

"*Your* problem?" Annie repeated, mentally cursing herself for losing another shootout at the Not-So-O.K. Corral. "What would it take to give you some faith in my abilities? A testimonial from Eliot Ness?"

Matt couldn't resist sliding his arm around her waist. "After everything that's happened, you just don't get it, do you?" he murmured. When she gave him a startled look, he released her and turned businesslike again. "Maybe during lunch you can jog my memory or ask a question I haven't asked myself. I really want to start to zero in on this nemesis of mine. He or she is becoming a real pest."

They lapsed into silence for the remainder of the walk, but Annie was acutely aware of Matt every step of the way. She felt as if he'd left his imprint on her body when he'd touched her, and each time his fingers accidentally brushed hers, her nerves leapt as if she'd grabbed a high-voltage wire.

At the park, Matt found them a picnic table under a shady tree, and Annie's eyes widened as he unpacked the basket, pulling out fresh fruit, creamy cheeses, French bread, herbed chicken breasts, and a bottle of chilled Chablis—along with crystal, china, and silver. "What do you do when you're trying to dazzle one of your dates?" she asked, her eyes dancing despite her puzzlement. "Hire a waiter in a tux, a strolling mariachi band, and a couple of flamenco dancers?"

Matt grinned. "Doesn't everybody?"

Annie shook her head and began to relax. Soon her senses came alive, as if physical pleasures were a whole new discovery for her. She luxuriated in the penetrating heat of the sun, smiled at the gurgle of a fountain, eavesdropped on the whispered secrets of a breeze riffling through the trees.

After the first course had stimulated her taste buds, Matt playfully held a juicy peach to her mouth, and she bit into it, giggling and catching the sweet nectar on her tongue before it could dribble down her chin. The Chablis he poured for her was a splash of icy tartness; a wedge of perfect Brie he held while she sank her teeth into it was soothingly ripe and creamy.

During one special moment of shared laughter

over a silly comment she'd made, Annie looked into Matt's eyes and lost herself in a blue-green universe. She was dizzy. She was exhilarated. She felt as if she were floating in a clear, brilliant sky. Matt didn't need dancers and a band, or any props at all, she thought, her heart thrumming out of control. He was dazzling on his own.

Even when she remembered to be businesslike and ask questions about certain employees, Annie felt an unprecedented warmth taking hold of her. Matt knew everyone who worked for the company, and had a knack of telling some amusing anecdote to show why this or that person couldn't possibly be a suspect. He was funny, he was kind, he was affectionate. She hardly noticed that he brushed aside her queries about Elizabeth Reynolds.

"I think you're wrong about something," she remarked.

"About what?" Matt asked, hoping Annie wasn't going to insist that one of the employees could be the letter writer.

She smiled. "About luck being the reason for your low staff turnover. You get loyalty because you give it, Matt."

"Thank you," he said quietly.

"Don't thank me. I'm just making an observation."

Matt shook his head. "I meant for using my first name. I was beginning to think you never would."

Annie was surprised she'd given up the formality without realizing it. And she was astonished that Matt seemed so pleased. "You haven't asked me to use your first name," she reminded him.

"Does a girl from Boston have to be asked?"

Annie laughed. "She does if she's been trained by Miss Effie."

"Who's Miss Effie?" Matt asked, his voice rich with amusement as he began clearing up the lunch debris, regretting how quickly the time had gone by. He always felt time flew when he was with Annie.

She pitched in to help. "Miss Effie Stanforth teaches deportment to young Boston ladies whose families still cling to the ways of the distant past. I hated going to her boring Saturday morning torture sessions, wandering around actually trying to balance a book on my head, when there was touch football going on outside."

Matt chuckled, somehow not surprised by Annie's preference. "Were you such a tomboy?"

The deep timbre of his voice aroused more stirrings in Annie. Dangerous ones. "I was a *hopeless* tomboy," she admitted too eagerly, as if trying to remind herself that she was too unfeminine to give in to the softness Matt made her feel. "My mother wouldn't hear of a Brentwood daughter growing up without learning the social graces from Miss Effie," she went on, by this time talking just to keep from dealing with what was happening inside her. "There wasn't enough money in the formerly fat Brentwood coffers for Swiss finishing schools. There was only a leftover conviction that we were Boston aristocrats and had to act the part. So off I went to Miss Effie, until she gave up on me. Poor lady. She called me her Lost Cause."

Matt was beginning to understand that Annie had had to fight hard to be her own person. "Your mother made you spend your Saturday mornings learning etiquette from Miss Effie," he mused aloud as he packed up the wicker basket. "And yet you ultimately became a private detective. It's not exactly the American blueblood's preferred choice of profession. Making it happen must have been tough."

Annie laughed, though she hadn't seen much humor in the family battles at the time. "Flunking teacup-lifting was hard enough to tell the folks. Refusing to play wide-eyed debutante just about got me disowned. But the explosion when I said I'd signed on at the cop shop—"

"The cop shop?" Matt cut in. "You started out as a policewoman?"

"It was my basic training. But I'm not too good with rules and bureaucracy, so my lieutenant suggested I might be happier working in private security, where I wouldn't keep getting promoted and then busted back to the beat for some dumb infraction. Yo-Yo Annie, they called me. Anyway, I went the insurance company route—investigating claims and such. At night I took some computer courses so . . ." She frowned. "How did you manage to get me talking about myself? We're supposed to discuss you, Mr. Harper."

"Annie, if you go back to using my last name, I just might whup you," Matt said pleasantly.

She laughed. "I wouldn't try it, boss."

"Come to think of it, maybe I won't. I remember what you did to Big Merv." Reluctantly getting to his feet, Matt held out his hand to Annie. "Let's go, Killer."

Entwining her fingers with his, Annie smiled. They did seem to have a real truce at last. A cease-fire, at least.

How long it would last was a question she didn't want to think about.

As it happened, the armistice ended within the hour.

Eight

Matt and Victoria were leaning on their flattened palms over his desk glaring at each other when a wide-eyed Josette showed Annie into Matt's office.

"No," Matt was saying to his mother. "No, Victoria. It stops here. It stops now."

"You'd overrule me?" Victoria demanded. "The board?"

Matt flinched slightly, then nodded. "I'll call a meeting and explain a few new details."

Annie frowned. Was Matt going to use his veto after all? Had he been nice to her at lunch only to turn around and fire her now? Clearing her throat, she made a bid for attention. "Did you send for me, Mr. Harper?"

His head shot up, and he aimed his furious gaze at her. "No, I did not send for you, Miss Brentwood."

"*I* did," Victoria said, drawing herself up to her full height and turning to smile reassuringly at Annie.

Annie wasn't surprised to see a glint of determination in the older woman's eyes. But there was also a puzzling twinkle of secret satisfaction.

"Annie, go away," Matt said evenly.

"Annie, don't you dare," Victoria countered. "You stay right here."

Down with the white flag and up with the battle standards, Annie thought. Go away, he'd said. After all that charm he'd poured on. Go away. She felt like an irritating gnat he'd taken a swipe at. And she was outraged. "Stay here. Go away. Stay here. Go away. Why don't you two just find a great big carving knife and call in your local Solomon?" she snapped. "Or, since this is cowboy country, maybe you'd like to tie me to a couple of wild stallions and send them racing off in opposite directions! What the hell's the matter now?"

Victoria straightened up, tipped back her head, and laughed uproariously. "Oh, I do like this woman," she said when she'd settled down.

"Well?" Annie demanded, folding her arms over her chest. She'd just about had it. How could she solve the stupid case, when she wasn't getting any help from the intended victim?

Realizing he'd lost all the ground he'd gained with Annie, Matt was livid with his mother. But he knew Annie would side with Victoria, so he was annoyed with her too. What really had him upset, though, was the thought of taking an overnight trip with Annie—without a chaperone. "I have to go to Fort Worth," he said, moving from behind his desk to stalk over to the bar in the sitting area. "I'm going alone," he added as he took out a glass and splashed bourbon into it.

"You are not going alone, you're taking Annie," Victoria said. "I've already made the arrangements for both of you. And while you're pouring, perhaps you might ask the ladies present if they would like a little something from the bar. I know I'd welcome a gin and tonic."

"Nothing for me, thank you," Annie said through gritted teeth, her patience badly strained. "My head's spinning enough as it is."

Matt got out some ice and another glass, and started preparing his mother's drink. "You can just get busy and unmake those arrangements, Victoria. I don't mind the last-minute trip. I'm willing to go to the cocktail party, and I'll even sit through the ballet. But I will not drag Annie along."

Annie opened her mouth to ask something, but didn't get past her first syllable.

"Matthew, do you really expect her to solve this case by sitting at a computer poring through files?" Victoria asked, striding to one of the black leather armchairs and lowering herself into it. "What can she learn tucked away in your apartment every night, not seeing you with friends or business acquaintances or anyone besides Judith? Annie has to watch you in action!"

"Do you think I'm a complete idiot?" Matt demanded as he handed his mother her drink. He plunked himself down on the couch and sat forward, his glass held loosely in his two hands while his elbows rested on his knees. "Cut out the act, Mother. We all know you haven't hired Annie to protect me or to play Polly Pinkerton and find out who's behind those letters. You've decided some woman is our villain, and Annie's presence will smoke her out. But I don't want to put Annie in that position. I don't want her around if your theory's correct. And you shouldn't want to put her in that position, either."

Annie tried again to speak. "But I knew—"

"Matthew," Victoria said sharply. "Annie knows why I want her on this case."

Exactly what I was going to say, Annie thought, getting a little tired of being ignored. "Mr. Harper, Victoria's telling—"

"I won't argue anymore," he said, then tossed back half his bourbon as if the gesture ended the discussion.

"Matthew, I'm really starting to—"

A long, shrill whistle stopped Victoria in mid-sentence.

Both Matt and Victoria turned to gape at Annie in time to see her thumb and index finger still at the corners of her mouth. She lowered her hand to her side. "Sorry," she said, not sounding the least bit apologetic. "It seemed to be the only way to get your attention."

Victoria grinned. "You know, I always wanted to learn to do that, but I never could. What's the trick? Is it all in the way you hold your lips? Is it the tongue?"

Matt's lips twitched in amusement, but he managed not to crack a smile. "I don't suppose Miss Effie taught you how to make that ungodly noise, Miss Brentwood."

"Who's Miss Effie?" Victoria said.

"Miss Effie of Boston taught Annie to be a lady," Matt drawled.

"Miss Effie," Annie said evenly, too fed up to care about consequences, "was no more successful in making a lady out of me than anyone else ever was. But she did pound it into my head that it's impolite to go on and on about people right in front of them as if they're not there. Will someone please tell me exactly what's up?"

Matthew and Victoria started talking at once, but stopped with matching winces when Annie raised her hand to her mouth again in a silent threat.

With a gesture of his hand, Matt backed off to let his mother speak first.

Victoria smiled at Annie. "Come and sit down, dear."

Moving slowly and guardedly, Annie made her way to the chair opposite Victoria's. "All right, I'm listening. What's this talk about Fort Worth?"

"I was scheduled to attend a benefit. A cocktail party and dinner at the Fort Worth Harper Plaza, followed by a ballet gala," Victoria explained. "Unfortunately, I've had to ask Matthew to go in my place while I baby-sit my grandchildren in Dallas. Mirella called me a little while ago because she sprained her ankle this—"

"She's always hurting herself," Matt grumbled. "Mirella can't just play a game of tennis. She goes on the attack, as if she thinks she's jousting."

"Rather like her brother," Victoria said pleasantly, then arched her brow. "Why do you seem to think a killer instinct is fine for you but not for your sisters?"

"Mirella doesn't have a killer instinct," Matt countered. "She has a suicidal urge. If she wants to play so hard, she should get in shape first. But no, she sits around for six months, watches a couple of exercise tapes and calls it a workout, then all of a sudden gets a spurt of ambition and hits the courts running. She's—"

"Matthew, don't you think we're getting a little off the topic here?" Victoria said with a long-suffering smile.

Annie was annoyed. She'd thought she'd found a fatal flaw in Matt's character—that he was just like her whole family, thinking all women should be demure and ladylike. But his comments about Mirella were reasonable; he wasn't being chauvinistic. She forced her attention back to the main issue. "When is this benefit?"

"Tonight," Matt and Victoria both answered.

Annie raised her brow. She wasn't crazy about last-minute curves in a protection assignment. "And how do you plan to get to Fort Worth? The *Cheyenne*?"

Matt nodded.

"Good. I can check it out fairly quickly."

"You're not coming with me," Matt said firmly. "I plan to take off for Fort Worth in three hours. Alone."

"You're not taking off anywhere until I've made certain the plane has been given more than a routine going-over," Annie shot back. "I thought I'd explained to you that there are all sorts of dandy little places on a private aircraft to plant altitude-sensitive explosives."

"You see, Matthew?" Victoria said, glaring at her son. "Annie is far more than a decoy. She's a knowledgeable security expert."

As Annie leapt up and headed for the door, Victoria said, "You'll need something spectacular to wear."

Annie stopped in her tracks and turned. "How spectacular?"

Instead of answering Annie directly, Victoria stood up and went to Matt's desk. She picked up a memo pad and pen and started jotting down a list. "Matthew, before you leave for Fort Worth I want you to take Annie shopping for a suitable drop-dead evening gown. I'm making a note of the boutique the girls and I use in the Galleria. Ask for Suzy; she's wonderfully helpful, and she knows how to handle the billing. Meanwhile, I'll call Fort Worth to get Annie an appointment at the salon in the hotel. Mr. Frederick will squeeze her in if I ask him to. Be sure you also buy the proper accessories—shoes, evening bag, jewelry. *Faux* will do. Suzy will find just the thing, I'm sure." Tearing off the sheet of paper with a flourish and marching over to hand it to Matt, she added, "Remember, this benefit is *the* social event of the year. Everybody who's anybody from all over the state will be there. We want our Annie to shine."

Matt glanced at Annie. He expected her to erupt in all-out fury at his mother's high-handedness. Maybe *now* she'd quit!

But Annie didn't look furious. She looked stunned. Frightened.

A smile suddenly tugged at Matt's lips. At last, he thought. At long last he'd found something that scared the woman. He'd located her Achilles' heel. "Okay, I give in," he said, tucking his mother's list into his inside breast pocket. "Annie can tag along. It's probably a great idea, come to think of it. She'll get to see a lot of people, watch their reactions to me, chat up at least half my acquaintances, pretend to be my latest lady love, and maybe even get a reaction from my secret admirer." He grinned. "Just think, Annie. Those Saturday mornings at Miss Effie will come in handy after all."

Annie finally found her voice. "Wait a minute," she said, the sound high and strangled. "I'm no good at this sort of thing."

"Hey, you're either my bodyguard or you're not," Matt pointed out, feeling almost sorry for her—but not enough to show mercy. "C'mon, Annie. Let's go."

"No," she said, shaking her head vigorously. "Uh-uh. Let's do some negotiating here, Mr. Harper. I'll take a bullet meant for you. I'll step between you and an assassin's oriental dagger. I'll dismantle a ticking time bomb. But don't ask me to play Barbie Goes to the Ballet!"

"You'll have to, Miss Brentwood," he insisted. "I've finally realized that my mother is right about the approach we've taken to solving this case. You can't do it from this computerized ivory tower. You've got to get out there and meet everybody I know, starting tonight. Then I'm going to arrange some parties at the apartment and a monster barbecue at the ranch. Maybe I should even make a date with each woman I've been out with for the past year—all suspects, remember—and let you tag along."

"Matthew," Victoria said in a warning tone.

Matt ignored her. "Go shut down your computer, Miss Brentwood. You and I are going shopping for fancy duds." Deliberately, he let his gaze roam over every delectable inch of Annie's body. "I think I'll pick something red and slinky for you. I want people to notice my escort. I want other men to envy me." To his surprise, he meant the last part of what he'd said. Every word. And his enthusiasm was only partly faked.

"Hold it, Henry Higgins!" Annie said, suspecting he was just baiting her but dubious enough to be terrified. "You've got the wrong Eliza Doolittle if you're going to turn this assignment into a coming-out party. I was Miss Effie's Lost Cause, remember?"

"Think of it this way, Annie," Matt said, moving toward her, thoroughly enjoying the renewal of the game. "Here's your chance to redeem yourself.

To show that you could make Miss Effie proud if you really tried. And what if my killer-to-be is at that benefit tonight? You wouldn't want to miss the chance to make her tip her hand."

Annie's knees threatened to buckle as Matt casually slid his arm around her shoulders and gave her a quick hug. She shot a desperate look at Victoria. "Could I just waste him, ma'am?" she pleaded. "Think about it. You wouldn't have to worry about him ever again if I did him in right now. I'll make it quick and painless. What do you say, Victoria?"

"Tempted as I am, I can't countenance the murder of my son," Victoria answered. "But I'll tell you this much, young lady: By the time my elves get through with you . . ." She grinned and her sea-blue eyes, so like Matt's, danced with wicked merriment. "Honey, you're gonna knock him dead."

Matt scowled at the desk clerk of the Fort Worth Harper Plaza. "What do you mean, only one room?"

The pallid young man studied his computer screen. "Not one room, Mr. Harper. One suite. It has two bedrooms. I'm sorry if there's been some . . . some breakdown in communications, but our records show that your mother booked her usual accommodations. And there simply isn't another room or suite available. We're bursting at the seams, thanks to all the conventions."

"I understand," Matt said quietly, signing the register. There was no point arguing; he knew the clerk was telling the truth, and pulling rank as an owner wasn't the Harper style. Victoria had stage-managed another coup.

Matt wondered what Annie's reaction to this development would be. He'd turned her over to Victoria's precious Mr. Frederick the minute they'd arrived, and she wasn't due out of the salon for about an hour. Probably she would cope perfectly well. She took her sentry duty seriously. Besides, except for a couple of notable lapses, Annie didn't seem to be suffering as intensely as he was from temptations that were becoming impossible to resist.

The truth was, Matt realized, his game had started backfiring the instant Annie had surrendered to the inevitability of going with him to Fort Worth. Once she'd given in, not even her obvious terror of haughty salesclerks would make her back down.

Then, when she'd emerged from the Galleria boutique's dressing room wearing the gown he'd picked out, Matt had known he was in for a rougher time than anything he could dish out to Annie.

He'd wanted red and slinky? He'd gotten it, and Annie's slim curves filled out the ankle-length silk jersey in a way even he hadn't envisioned. And the high-heeled, strappy red sandals Suzy had come up with were dangerous to a man's sanity, at least on Annie's delicately arched feet.

Matt had nodded his approval of the outfit, wondering if his X-rated thoughts were obvious. He'd begun to have serious doubts that he could get through an entire evening pretending he was a civilized man.

Then, without warning, he'd found himself completely caught up in the shopping expedition. Matt Harper, who'd never been inside a boutique in his life, had been carried away by the unexpected, intimate pleasure of playing Pygmalion. Not only had he taken Suzy aside and pointed to some lacy lingerie and real silk stockings for Annie, he'd decided that *faux* simply meant fake, and fake wasn't good enough. He'd called a Fort Worth jeweler to order a genuine version of the kind of starburst brooch and earrings Suzy had suggested to complement the dress.

Not one of his efforts, he'd realized with a shock, had been part of a game.

Annie had seemed dazed until they'd reached the Cheyenne and, dressed again in her own no-nonsense outfit, she'd swung into action like a real pro, going over an incredibly detailed check-list to make sure the plane was safe. During the flight she'd maintained a businesslike detachment, hitting Matt with a barrage of crisp questions about all sorts of people in his life.

He'd been amazed by how much she'd learned about him during the past couple of weeks—and by how little he really knew about her. It was an imbalance he intended to correct as soon as possible.

And now, it seemed, he wasn't faced with trying just to get through an evening with a woman his body responded to with a deep, throbbing ache; he was looking at an entire night alone with her.

"It's happening just the way I knew it would," Matt said to Annie as they stood under a crystal chandelier sipping champagne at the gala cocktail party. "All the men are envious of me."

"If you're trying to make me feel self-conscious, Mr. Harper," she said, "forget it. I've gotten over my initial panic. If bullying me into going undercover as a coporate moll hasn't sent me scurrying for cover, nothing will."

"A corporate moll?" Matt repeated, laughing. "Does that make me the Al Capone of Houston's business community?"

Annie shrugged. "If the spats fit . . ."

Matt laughed again. "Honey, however this night started out, I'm glad you've gotten over your panic. You're turning what could have been a dreary evening into the most fun I've had since my father first taught me to rope a calf."

Suspecting that he was still just roping a calf, and that she was the little heifer about to be brought down, Annie steeled herself against softening. "Who's that blonde standing over there to the left of the cellist?" she asked abruptly.

Matt followed the direction of Annie's glance. "Her name's Diana Young. Why do you ask?"

"I keep catching her staring at me," Annie answered, then smiled sweetly. "Is she one of yours?"

To his horror, Matt felt a flush rising over his skin. It irritated him that Annie had a perfect right to ask him the question. "I took Diana out once," he muttered.

"Only once?"

He nodded grudgingly. "Okay, maybe twice. Look, you're new to this scene, Annie. People are curious, that's all. Diana isn't jealous; she's not shooting green daggers your way. Nobody is."

"Maybe you're right," Annie conceded. "After all, from what I've gathered, I wouldn't become target practice until after the third time I'd been seen with you." Annie smiled. "By the way what do you know about one Elizabeth Reynolds?"

"Cool it, Annie," he snapped. "This isn't the time or place for *This Is Your Life.*"

Annie laughed. "You really do watch some ancient shows, Mr. Harper. And so *many* of them." Her glance moved over his lean, hard body. "Funny, you don't look like a couch potato," she added in a low undertone.

Matt felt a familiar heat rising through him. Annie's eyes, he decided, were lethal. And as far as he could tell, she had no idea of their power. "What *do* I look like, Annie?"

Only when he spoke did Annie realize she'd made her observation aloud. How awful, she thought furiously. Her irrepressible lust was showing. What was it about Matt Harper that had turned her into a shameless predator? She'd never been so unprofessional—or so boldly sensual—in her entire life!

Annie made up her mind that bluntness was the only way to handle the situation. "You look like the most eligible bachelor in the entire state, Mr. Harper—which, I'm sure you're aware, is exactly what you are. Apart from your insufferable cockiness, you're quite an attractive specimen, as roosters go, so it's natural that all the other hens are ready to peck out my eyes. What I don't understand is why you're so set against talking to me about the chicks on my list of suspects."

"Because I . . . because . . ." Suddenly realizing he'd given Annie the upper hand, Matt decided to take it back and keep it, come hell or high water. He allowed his smile to suggest what he was feeling, and slid his arm around her to feather his fingertips over her back. "C'mon, Annie," he said, his tone softening to a caress as he felt her shiver and saw the flames of desire that instantly flared in her eyes. "You're a detective, sweetheart. Isn't it time you figured out why I don't want to talk to you about other women?"

Annie tipped back her head and stared up at him for a long, tense moment as her common sense battled the guerrilla forces that were bent on toppling it. "You don't fight fair," she whispered.

Matt slowly wagged his head from side to side. "Maybe I'm not fighting at all, Annie." He had no trouble making his comment believable.

She swallowed hard and, when one of Matt's many friends came over to speak to them, she gave a silent, long-overdue thanks to Miss Effie and those awful Saturday morning classes in the art of mindless small talk.

Nine

"You were wonderful," Matt said as he unlocked the door to the hotel suite. "No company president ever had a more charming corporate moll on his arm."

"The benefit was great," Annie said, wishing she didn't have to sound so strangled.

"And?" Matt prompted, opening the door and letting Annie go in ahead of him.

Annie searched wildly for something innocuous to say. "And the gala!" she almost shouted. "It was fantastic! Every number was one of my favorites. The scenes from *Giselle* from . . ." Vaguely noticing that Matt had closed the door but wasn't flicking on the light switch, Annie strode to the huge picture window to stand looking out at Fort Worth's glittering skyline, her heart beginning to pound out a primitive, syncopated rhythm. "I'd forgotten how much I love the ballet," she half-whispered.

Matt stayed just inside the door, drinking in Annie's moonlit loveliness, aware of a new kind of warmth pervading his being, as if something that had been frozen deep inside him for years was starting to thaw like a mountain stream at

March breakup. Annie, he said silently. Annie, his own special breath of spring.

He smiled, aware that Annie knew what was about to happen, whether she'd admitted it to herself or not. She was still fighting the inevitable—and she was endearingly nervous. He didn't blame her. He was a little nervous himself. For the first time in his life, he was about to walk off the edge of an emotional precipice, with no idea where he was going to land. "You surprise me," he teased, trying to slice through the thick tension.

"Why?" Annie asked in a small voice.

Matt chuckled and moved toward her. "A Lost Cause tomboy who likes the ballet?" he murmured as he spanned her slender waist with his hands. "I never know quite what to expect from you, Annie."

A fiery liquid began moving slowly but inexorably through her body, starting at the point of contact with his hands and radiating into every nook and cranny of her being. Surrender, she thought with fearful excitement, was imminent. She wanted to welcome it. To lean back against Matt's strong body and give in to the pleasure of his gentle caresses. To forget that she was being a fool, to ignore the fact that she might be just another conquest to him.

Her body stiffened as she made a last, shaky effort to resist. The only defense left to her, she thought helplessly, was mindless chatter. Perhaps she could bore him to distraction. "When I was little," she said with a ragged laugh, "I couldn't decide whether I wanted to earn my quarterback jersey or my tutu and toe shoes. Somehow I'd gotten the idea that eventually I'd get to pick which sex I wanted to be when I grew up. I wasn't sure what to choose: Guys seemed to have most of the fun, but girls got to be glamorous and pretty and . . ."

"I'm glad you made the right choice when the time came," Matt said, dipping his head to brush his lips over Annie's temple, then the delicate skin in front of her ear.

"I did?" Annie said on a sigh. Shuddering with delight, she instinctively tilted her head to give Matt easier access. "What about your rules, Mr. Harper?" she whispered.

Matt traced her ear's outer rim with the tip of his tongue, his hands tightening around her waist. "What rules?" he asked, his voice low and husky.

Annie didn't answer for a moment. She was having trouble thinking. "Your rules about . . . about messing with employees," she said at last. "Have you forgotten them?"

"I'm breaking them," Matt answered calmly. "And I'm not messing with you, Annie." He turned her to face him and cradled her face between his two hands. "I'm making love to you."

Annie gazed up at him, transfixed. "Oh dear," she murmured after a long, long moment.

Matt smiled, bemused by the way her eyes could smolder with erotic eagerness, yet flicker with anxiety. "What are you afraid of, Annie?" he asked gently.

"Everything," she blurted out.

"I don't believe it. My intrepid Annie, afraid?" The truth was, Matt had a good idea what at least one of Annie's fears was. Considering what she knew—or thought she knew—about his reputed love-'em-and-leave-'em track record, not to mention his motives in making love to her, she had every right to be uneasy. "It's your call, Annie," he said, his gaze locked on hers. "Do you want me to back off?"

Annie's thoughts whirled. Here was her chance, she told herself. All she had to do was nod her head. She didn't even have to say anything. Matt wouldn't push, wouldn't coerce, wouldn't coax. Somehow she knew he would respect her answer, whatever it was. And the freedom he gave her to make her own decision was what ultimately disarmed her. "I should want you to back off, Matt," she said at last. "But heaven help me, I don't. I just . . . I just want you."

Smiling to hide a relief so enormous it astounded him, Matt reached up to take the combs from Annie's hair and pocket them, then plunged his fingers into the thick, silky strands he'd released, enjoying the sheer tactile pleasure of their rich texture. "Talk to me," he murmured, touching his lips to her forehead, her brows, her closed eyelids. "Tell me why you should want me to back off. The real reason, not the red herrings we've both been using to avoid facing what we feel."

Sliding her hands under Matt's jacket and flattening her palms against his chest, Annie realized his heart was pounding as wildly as her own. "If you really want to know, let's get the clichés out of the way first," she said with a tiny smile, emboldened by his emotional response. "To begin with, I'm afraid I'll hate myself in the morning."

"I won't let you," Matt answered. "I won't give you a chance to hate yourself in the morning or any other time."

Annie smiled, oddly certain he meant it—at

least right now. And wasn't right now enough? Did she need to ask for more?

She reached up to trace his rugged features with her fingertips. "You're really kind of sweet, Matt Harper."

"For a cocky rooster," he said, closing his eyes and reveling in Annie's touch. "Does your discovery that I'm a sweet guy calm your fears?" he remembered to ask a moment later. "Or is there anything else that scares you? Let's get it all out of the way."

Annie was amazed by the sudden thickness of his voice, the tremor that went through his body. Was it possible, she wondered, that her impact on Matt was as powerful as his on her? That he was as moved as she was? How silly, she told herself, remembering the gorgeous blonde named after a Greek goddess. The lovely Diana had rated only one date—or maybe two—with Matt Harper. What chance could an awkward puritan have of meaning something more to him than another passing amusement? "My inexperience gives me some pause," she confessed impulsively, resting her hands on his shoulders. "I mean, I'm not suggesting I've never . . . It's just that . . . well, I'm not exactly . . . an *expert*." She managed a self-conscious laugh. "Remember me? I'm the grubby-faced Eliza who never became a lady. I'm the buddy all the boys confided in, not the girl they dreamed about." She laughed again and shook her head, suddenly feeling utterly ridiculous. "I'm a fighter, Matt, not a lover."

Matt opened his eyes and grinned at her. "Wrong, sweetheart. I always did like Eliza better before she turned into a lady. And *you're* the woman I've been dreaming about. My buddy, my feisty little fighter, and my lover, because those brown eyes of yours have been making love to me."

"They have?" Annie said, startled to find out she'd been so obvious.

Matt laughed quietly. "When they weren't spitting fire, that is." Taking one of her hands in his, he brought the tips of her fingers to his lips, kissing each in turn, then brushed his mouth over her palm, following the fortune lines with his tongue. "Annie, only the sweetest of lovers could do what your hands did to me a moment ago, just by touching my face. When I think what they'll do . . ." He let his words die away, leaving the rest to Annie's imagination as he released her hand and began trailing kisses along her delicate jawline and over her slender, arched throat. "But I don't think it's your inexperience that bothers you," he added after several pleasurable minutes, deciding after all to take a chance on bringing the real issue out into the open, "as much as what you believe is my experience."

Strange, Annie thought as his warm breath fanned her skin, she hadn't known about the invisible fuses that seemed to connect countless explosive nerve centers in her body, yet Matt knew exactly how and where to find the detonators. "The truth is, I think I'm counting on your experience," she said, her fears washed away by the fast-rising tide of her desire.

Matt lifted his head to gaze at her. "And I think the *real* truth is that we're both babes in the woods when it comes to what's happening between us."

"Do you always have to add some amendment to whatever I say?" Annie mumbled teasingly, unprepared to deal with what Matt seemed to be suggesting.

"Probably," he answered gravely. "And that's just one of the land mines ahead for us, Annie."

Every part of her being wanted him to clarify exactly what he was saying, yet at the same time shrank from it. As usual, Annie took refuge in light banter. "And must you always have the last word, Mr. Harper?"

Matt gave her a lazy grin. "Depends what the last word is."

"Meaning?"

"If the last word is *yes*," Matt said, lowering his mouth to hers. "I want it to be yours."

Annie hesitated only for an instant, then murmured against his warm, firm lips. "Then the last word is mine."

They shared a slow, delicious kiss charged with all the need and longing that had been building between them. Gradually the intimacy deepened. Lips parted, tongues met, tasted, stroked, explored in a release of the suppressed yearnings of a lifetime.

It felt unbelievably right to Annie when Matt's hands moved to her shoulders and slid downward, slowly inching toward her breasts until he gently cupped them. Their tips pressed eagerly against the thin silk of her gown, seeking his palms. "Annie," Matt whispered. "Where did you come from all of a sudden?"

"Boston," she automatically answered, too dazed to know what she was saying.

"I know," Matt said, chuckling. He circled her swollen nipples with his thumbs, arousing them, making them stand at rigid, pouting attention. "Beautiful. Banned-in-Boston Annie. But I wasn't talking about hometowns, sweetheart. I guess I'm trying to figure out how you strolled into my life and zapped me in a way I've never been zapped before."

"I didn't," Annie said, desperately trying to keep one foot on the ground while she allowed the rest of herself to soar. "Tonight's just tonight," she said bravely, "and it's enough for me. I know I'm an illusion, Matt, and you should know it too, because I'm your own handiwork. You sprinkled magic dust and turned me into a mysterious lady in red—with a little help from Victoria's elves—and you mustn't lose sight of the fact that tomorrow I'll be just Annie again."

Matt raised his hands to her shoulders and slowly shook his head. "Listen to me, my blind-folded little private eye. No woman was ever less of an illusion to me. I enjoyed sprinkling magic dust today, if that's what you want to call the fun we had. But *you* excite me. You. Not the Mr. Frederick hairdo or the red dress or the sexy shoes. . . ." He stopped and grinned wickedly. "Well, maybe the shoes."

Annie gave a throaty laugh and twined her arms around his neck. "You really like the red shoes, huh?"

"Yeah. I really like the red shoes." Matt's grin faded. "But let me show you what I like a whole lot better." Reaching behind his neck, he took Annie's hands, then moved her away from the window. "I know the room is dim, and we're on the top floor, but I want total privacy for what I have in mind," he said quietly. Releasing her hands, he slipped his fingers under the neckline of her gown and pushed the soft jersey material downward. "Just Annie, you call yourself?" he murmured as he bent to blaze a trail of kisses across each graceful curve of bared shoulder. "Just Annie is the woman I've wanted all along."

She offered no more resistance than her dress did as Matt gradually peeled it from her body until she was naked to the waist. Lavishing kisses on every inch of creamy skin he exposed, he murmured constantly how beautiful she was. He smoothed his palms over her back, her arms, her torso, then cupped her breasts again and gently squeezed them, dipping his head to take each protruding, shell-pink nipple into his mouth and tease it to the rosy, swollen perfection of a juicy berry.

Annie began to feel beautiful and feminine and gloriously sensual. Arching her back, she abandoned herself to Matt's sweet torment, happily stepping out of her gown when he pushed it over her hips and it landed in a soft heap on the floor.

"Perfect," Matt said, his eyes dark and smoldering as she stood before him in wisps of scarlet silk and lace, her legs slim and shapely in sheer black stockings held up by satin garters, her slender feet showcased in shoes made for anything but walking.

As he saw a flush spread over her pale skin, watched her tongue moisten her parted lips, exulted in the way his mouth had shaped and reddened the tips of her breasts, he felt a tide of primitive male triumph wash over him. Annie had been right, he mused. In a way, she *was* his handiwork. He was nurturing her exquisite womanliness. Taming the tomboy. "Miss Effie," he said slowly, sweeping Annie up in his arms, "just didn't have access to the right techniques."

Annie twined her arms around his neck and

nuzzled into the fragrant warmth of his throat. She knew exactly what he meant, and instead of minding his masculine crowing she delighted in it. If Matt had been around when she'd been debating whether to grow up to be male or female, she suspected, there'd have been no contest. Touch football wouldn't have stood a chance.

Matt carried her to his room and lowered her to the king-size bed, the covers already turned back by the chambermaid while they'd been out. He recaptured Annie's mouth in a long, deep, possessive kiss, then released her and straightened up. "I think it's time for me to slip into something more comfortable," he said, beginning to loosen his tie.

"Shouldn't I take off my shoes?" Annie suggested playfully.

Shrugging out of his jacket and hanging it on the wooden valet, Matt grinned. "Not yet, sweetheart. I'll get to them, and everything else that isn't just Annie. But for now I'm enjoying the way you look."

"And I enjoy the way *you* look," Annie said, stretching languidly as she watched Matt undo his cuff links and shirt studs. "I have a feeling I'm going to enjoy it more by the minute."

"You ought to know," Matt said, his eyes twinkling with mischievous challenge. "You've been undressing me since the moment we met."

"I have not."

"It's all right," Matt assured her as he stripped off his shirt. "I've been doing the same to you."

Catching her breath as she watched the play of muscles under his bronze skin, Annie murmured, "You're a beast, Matt Harper. An arrogant, shameless, male beast." Her protest somehow sounded, even to her own ears, more like a compliment than a reprimand.

Within moments he'd stripped off the remainder of his clothes and was moving toward the bed.

"A gorgeous, arrogant, shameless, magnificent, male beast," Annie whispered as Matt stretched out beside her.

As he pulled her close, molding her soft curves to him, Annie felt the heat of him pressing into her, his hard masculinity throbbing with raw urgency. He kissed her in a way she'd never experienced before, part tenderness, part fierce demand, mercilessly and overwhelmingly possessive. Slipping one hand between their bodies, he stroked her breasts, her belly, bringing her to a fever of desire even before his fingers slid under the bit of crimson satin, thrust through her dark, soft triangle, and unerringly found the pulsating epicenter of her need. She clung to him, moaning helplessly, hardly aware she was begging for release, reaching down to curl her fingers around him in her own wordless demand.

Matt gasped with sudden pleasure. As always, he thought vaguely, Annie was turning the tables on him. And he loved her for it.

Ultimately he wasn't sure whether he moved over her of his own free will or she urged him to it. He wasn't sure whether he filled her because he couldn't hold back or because Annie's legs, wrapped around his hips, brought him into her welcoming warmth. He only knew that they were fused and moving as one, in a rhythm as old as time.

The next few hours were a maelstrom of undreamed-of pleasure for Annie. Matt loved her again and again, as if unable to get enough of her. He let her rest while he went to the master bathroom and filled the oversize sunken tub, then picked her up and chased away her sleepiness in the hot, steamy water. Lifting her to the side of the tub, he brought her to new heights of ecstasy before carrying her back to bed to love her again.

By the time she fell asleep just before dawn, tenderly cradled in Matt's arms, he knew her with an intimacy she'd never dreamed possible. He'd permitted her no secrets whatsoever; he'd stripped her of every shred of modesty and inhibition, until there was nothing more he could do to make her his.

Or so Annie thought.

When they woke to the sun streaming through the window, he began again, this time in the full light of day. "There'll be no shyness between us," he said quietly when she hesitated. "Not now, not ever."

Annie couldn't find the courage to ask him exactly what he meant. Despite everything they'd shared, she couldn't accept the exhilarating, terrifying possibility that Matt Harper felt something more for her than desire.

"There's something I've been wanting to discuss with you," Matt said as he and Annie got ready to return to Houston. After a shower together he'd given her the first turn at the hair dryer, so she was dressed and sitting at the vanity doing her makeup while he was getting into his clothes. "Why did you ask me about Elizabeth Reynolds last night?"

Annie, brushing brown shadow over her eyelids, slipped and managed to swipe the sponge-tipped applicator across the bridge of her nose. Grabbing a tissue to wipe off the smudge, she stared into the mirror at Matt, jarred from the languid contentment of a moment earlier. If he was prepared at last to answer her questions about the women in his life, she thought with a prickle of dread, he could have had better timing. But maybe he wanted to break the romantic spell before she started believing it.

She refused to act like an emotional bumpkin, even if she was one. Matt wanted a sophisticated woman? He'd get a super-sophisticated woman. "I'm sure I'm just reaching," she answered, returning to her task.

Matt wondered why Annie seemed to have cooled off by several degrees in a matter of seconds. Then he realized what was wrong: She still thought he was going to leave her now that he'd loved her. As usual, she was going to be feisty about the situation. No sad songs for Annie, he thought with a rush of affection. He was tempted to take her back to bed and show her how wrong she was, but it was ten-thirty and he'd filed a flight plan with a noon takeoff. Besides, teaching Annie that he was sincere and that his feelings would last—after all the games he'd been playing with her and his playboy reputation—would take serious concentration. He wanted to get the irritating matter of the mystery out of the way first. "What do you mean, you're just reaching?" he asked.

Annie shrugged. "I want so much to figure out who's writing you those letters, I tend to fasten on the slightest reason to suspect someone, that's all."

"And you're taking a second look at Elizabeth,"

Matt said, doing up his shirt buttons and watching with fascination as Annie picked up her mascara wand and swept it over her lashes with easy expertise. Strange, he mused. He'd never paid much attention to feminine rituals when his sisters had performed them. Or when anyone else had, for that matter. Yet everything Annie did was intriguing to him. "Why?" he asked, then clarified the question for himself as well as for Annie. "Why does Elizabeth seem to have captured your attention?"

"I'll tell you only if you promise not to make fun of me," Annie said.

He held up one hand as if taking an oath. "You've got my word on it, Pilgrim. Now, what did Elizabeth Reynolds do to catch your suspicious eye?"

While Matt continued dressing and Annie put the last touches on her makeup, she told him about the elements in the employee files that had put Elizabeth on her list of people to be checked out. Then, hesitantly, she mentioned the women's fleeting, hate-filled glance. To her surprise, Matt didn't tell her she was being ridiculous. He lapsed into deep thought. "You're not laughing," she said almost accusingly, packing her small cosmetic bag.

"I promised I wouldn't," he reminded her.

Annie rolled her eyes. "That wouldn't stop you."

"Thanks," Matt said, affecting a wounded look even though he had to admit he probably *would* have chuckled a little if a sudden, strange memory hadn't popped into his mind. "It's nice to know you have so much faith in me, my love. But there is a reason I'm not laughing."

All at once Annie didn't want to know. She

didn't want to hear him say that he and Elizabeth had been an item once, that his bodyguard wasn't the first employee who'd inspired him to break his rules.

"You know, you've got to work on your poker face if you want to stay in the gumshoe business," Matt said, curving his hands around Annie's shoulders and smiling into the mirror at her. "You're so transparent," he said, dropping a light kiss to the top of her head.

So much for being sophisticated, Annie thought. "What do you mean, I'm transparent?" she asked.

"You know what I mean, Annie," Matt answered, giving her a little squeeze and moving away to finish dressing before he forgot the demands of the outside world and started undressing again. Annie's eyes, he thought. They'd had a strange power over him since the beginning; he suspected they always would. "Now, about Elizabeth," he said with an effort, taking refuge in his most businesslike tone. "It doesn't make any sense that she would write those letters. I grew up with her husband. Joe Reynolds and I weren't great friends, but we'd known each other since high school, so when he got into some trouble about a year ago and came to me, I did him a favor."

"What favor?"

"Joe was fond of the track," Matt explained. "He had a habit of disappearing from time to time, following the horses around the country. Inevitably, he managed to dig himself into a financial hole he couldn't climb back out of. He came to me one afternoon for money. Apparently he had to come up with twenty thousand dollars before midnight or he was fish food." Matt paused, reflecting that he was starting to sound like

Annie, then went on. "I didn't think it was a great idea to help the guy—it seemed like giving an alcoholic a drink—but I couldn't turn my back on him. When he admitted he had an addiction, promised to go for counseling, and said he could repay me within the week, I made the loan. Joe was good for it; he paid me back within three days."

"Have you any idea how?" Annie asked, mentally reviewing a long string of similiar cases she'd worked on or heard about.

"I didn't at the time. But six months later, Joe skipped town, left Elizabeth and everything he owned—or rather, didn't own. It seemed he'd put a second mortgage on their house to come up with the twenty thousand. Elizabeth couldn't carry the debt load, and she lost everything. I felt guilty, so I went to her and offered to help. She wouldn't take anything but a job. She was pretty devastated, but she seemed to have a lot of pride."

Annie digested that information for a few moments. "Did you and Elizabeth talk about the loan you'd made to Joe?" she asked.

"Not really," Matt said after some thought. "I told her I felt a certain amount of responsibility for her situation, but she didn't seem to want to talk about it. She must have known the whole story; Joe told me that the house was in her name as well as his, so she'd have agreed to the mortgage deal."

"And then he left her high and dry," Annie murmured, quickly putting a few missing pieces together. The story was almost a classic. She wondered what version Joe had told Elizabeth. "Nice guy," she added, shaking her head.

"Hold it, Annie," Matt said hastily. "You are *not*

going to volunteer to track him down for Elizabeth. You already have a client, remember?"

"Do I?" she asked, getting up to take her purse from the closet shelf and slip her makeup pouch into it. "After last night, I think my only recourse is to turn in my Dear Boss letter."

Joining her at the closet to shrug into his suit jacket, Matt raised one brow quizzically. "Why?"

Annie turned to face him. "Because I dread confessing to your mother again, and this time having to tell her I literally ended up lying down on the job, that's why!"

"You don't have to confess anything to Victoria, Annie. I think some matchmaking has been part of her agenda all along."

Annie frowned, no longer sure what to believe about anything. "Now I'm confused. Do you, or do you not, want me off the case?"

"I did. But now wouldn't be a good time for you to quit."

"It wouldn't?"

"Not when it looks as if you're closing in on our culprit, sweetheart."

Annie's scowl deepened. "You mean Elizabeth?"

"Possibly. I don't know. I can't figure out why she'd turn on me after I tried to help, but remember that yellow Bonneville? The one I've been kidding you about. I don't think I'll kid you anymore."

Annie held her breath. "Why not?" she asked softly.

"Because I just remembered that Joe Reynolds drove a yellow Bonneville. He must have left it behind along with everything else. When I went to see Elizabeth, I think I remember seeing it in her driveway. I feel sorry for Elizabeth. I don't like facing the possibility that she'd turned her anger on me."

"Maybe she thinks she has reason," Annie said, more to herself than to Matt.

"Could be, I suppose," Matt conceded. "But it seems, Samantha Spade, that I owe you a few apologies. It turns out that you're a pretty good shamus after all. A real pro, just like Charlie said."

Annie smiled vaguely. Some pro, she thought. Since when did a real pro fall in love with the client?

Ten

"He *what*?" Annie yelped into the phone the following Wednesday at two o'clock. She'd just been through several days and nights of sweet but terrifying torture, and Charlie Dunhill wasn't coming to her rescue.

Charlie laughed. "Listen, don't ask me to explain it. All I know is that when I phoned you a while ago to tell you Rick Wallace was available at last to spell you off at night, I was put through to Matt instead. Seems like he'd left orders with the receptionist. I told him Rick would be his after-hours bodyguard from now on, and all of a sudden it was uh-uh. Annie's doing just fine, the man said. It's too late in the case to bring in an outsider, he told me. And Victoria gets really huffy at the slightest suggestion of replacing you, and we don't want to make Victoria huffy. Those Harpers, Annie. I'm telling you, you never know what to expect from them."

"No," Annie murmured, her heart pounding with fury and dread. "You just never know."

After she'd wished Charlie well with whatever nurse he had a crush on at the moment, Annie hung up, stared at the phone as if it were part of a conspiracy, then pushed herself away from her desk and got up to march to Matt's office.

"Josette, I'd like to speak to Mr. Harper," she said to the secretary.

Josette gave her an innocent smile. "He said you probably would, Annie. This special project you two are working on must be touchy. You're always at each other's throats."

Annie rolled her eyes and nodded. At each other's throats, she repeated silently. If only they could have limited themselves to throats, things might not have gotten so complicated.

"Annie's here," Josette said cheerfully as she opened Matt's door. "Lookin' just as riled as you said she would."

He stood up and grinned, but seemed to Annie to be braced for trouble. She gave it to him as soon as Josette had left them alone. "Why did you tell Charlie I couldn't be replaced? What am I, your slave?"

Without letting his smile waver even a little, Matt sat back down and nodded. "Slave?" he said. "Mmm. Has a nice ring to it. I'll even give you a new name, since you seem to feel cheated by your own. Something exotic. How about Shalimar? Maybe I'll make you dance for me."

"You've been making me dance for you for some time," Annie said. "Let up with the sexy charm, will you? You have no right to refuse to have Rick give me a hand on this job's graveyard shift. No right at all!"

"Graveyard shift?" Matt repeated, his smile tightening a little. "I didn't realize you were so unhappy with that shift."

"You're being as stubborn about this case as ever!" Annie shouted, then realized she was losing her dignity and lowered her voice. "We're almost positive Elizabeth is writing those letters, following you around," and getting closer and closer to making a potentially lethal move, and you won't let me do anything about it."

"Everything we have is purely circumstantial, Annie," Matt said evenly.

"We're not in a court of law, Mr. Harper, we're trying to keep you in one piece! At least, *I'm* trying to keep you in one piece. You're just extremely *trying!*" Starting to tremble with outrage, Annie sank into the chair in front of Matt's desk, then jumped up and started pacing again. "You make a lot of decisions all on your own. I don't remember being warned that your aunt was being relieved of her chaperone duties."

Matt steepled his fingers and lightly tapped them against his lower lip, sure he knew the real reason for Annie's anger and suspecting they were just getting to it now. "The whole family's going to be at the ranch this weekend for a traditional spring barbecue," he said quietly. "Aunt Judith always supervises the planning of the party. She offered to find someone else to stay with us, Annie, but somehow I didn't think you'd mind being alone with me."

Annie blinked rapidly as she felt her eyes filling with tears. The whole trouble, she wanted to tell Matt, was that she didn't mind at all. She liked being alone with him far too much. She was getting used to going home with him, sharing cooking chores as they taught each other their most outrageously spicy recipes, then going out from one romantic spot to another in Houston, finally returning to the apartment to make love until they were both exhausted enough to fall asleep in each other's arms. But Annie knew that she'd pay for every moment of pleasure with weeks of pain when the job was over and she and Matt resumed their normal lives. Even his own mother had pointed out his compulsion to move from relationship to relationship. She had to end this charade before she started believing in it. "And what's the point of all this . . . this sightseeing you've been subjecting me to?" she asked, turning away from Matt as she realized he was studying her with unnerving intensity.

"I've been trying to interrupt your countdown," he answered.

Annie sniffed back her tears. "What are you talking about?"

"You've pegged the remaining time on your office lease practically to the hour when you can pack your bags and leave this town, Annie," Matt said, getting to his feet and moving toward her. "You're in NASA territory, sweetheart. We know all about countdowns. I figured it was time for Houston Control to do whatever it took to put yours on hold. So I've been trying to show you how pleasant our fair city can be."

Annie began pacing again, trying to put some distance between them. She was well past the three-date limit Victoria had claimed he imposed on his relationships, yet he was talking as if he wanted her to still be around in ten months. "Your Texas pride has been stung, has it?" she said, grasping at the only explanation that seemed probable. "You think this state is the only one worth living in, and you can't stand the idea that someone might be happier in . . . in Rhode Island!"

"I don't think Texas is the only state worth living in," Matt said, still stalking Annie. "I think Texas is the only *place* in the world worth living in. And you'll feel the same way, sweetheart, if you'll just give yourself a chance."

"Don't call me *sweetheart*!" Annie cried.

Matt halted his advance, deciding to give Annie some breathing space. She was in a full-fledged panic, and he wanted to believe he knew why. He'd had a few scary moments himself when he'd realized what was happening between them. "You seemed to like that endearment last night," he reminded her.

"Well, I shouldn't have liked it. But you . . . you make me forget." She swallowed hard and took a deep breath. "Let's get back to the original issue here," she finally managed. "You had no right to refuse to see Rick Wallace. He's an excellent detective, and I want his help."

Matt gazed at her for a long moment. "I had ever right, and a very good reason, Annie." He went to his desk, picked up a letter, and held it out to her. "This came with the morning mail. The envelope had no stamp and no postmark. Obviously it was hand-delivered."

Annie snatched the paper from him.

"I'm not too crazy about this development," Matt said as she scanned the letter's contents.

Annie's eyes widened. "Our decoy plan seems to have worked," she said when she'd finished reading.

"I wouldn't say so," Matt remarked. "The idea was that having you on the scene might trigger an open attack against me. There wasn't supposed to be a switch making you the target. If ever I needed proof that I should have put the kibosh on the whole thing right from the start, this threat to you does it."

"Why?" Annie said with a lift of her chin. "This twist is perfect. Now I have the right to insist on bringing things to a head. And I'm not sure whether you've noticed, but this little note wasn't cranked out on the same old typewriter. This one was done on a computer. I'd be very surprised if Elizabeth didn't do this. Before you start playing Perry Mason, Mr. Harper, let me remind you that I'm now the intended victim, and this much circumstantial evidence is good enough for me. I'm going to get to the bottom of this mess before the day is out." Folding the letter and shoving it into the pocket of her khaki jacket, Annie turned on her heel and started toward the door.

"You'll do nothing of the sort!" Matt said, striding after her. He curled his fingers around her upper arm and whirled her to face him. "I have a meeting ten minutes from now with my banker and my accountant. It'll probably last most of the afternoon. I want you there."

"I've met your banker and your accountant. I've run a check on each of them. They're clear. I don't need to be at that meeting. And I have things to do. At the very least, I want to get some documents Elizabeth has worked on and take a look at the typefaces."

"Annie . . ."

"Don't push me, Mr. Harper," she said fiercely. "Maybe your Texas belles put up with your macho bossiness, but this Boston bean will push back."

Matt took a deep breath and let it out slowly. "All right. Fine. Check the damn typefaces. But you go to your office and stay away from Elizabeth, understand? We'll talk strategy tonight."

"If I haven't solved this case by five o'clock, your only company tonight will be Rick Wallace," Annie shot back. "I'm going to call Charlie right now."

"Forget it, Annie. If I have to pick you up and carry you, you're not going anywhere without me."

"Who's the bodyguard here, anyway?" Annie said fiercely. "You or me?"

Matt suddenly grinned, realizing for the first time the irony of the situation. "Both of us, baby," he said softly. "We have to guard each other's bodies. And since yours has become so precious to me, will you please refrain from indulging in Miss Marple heroics? Tomorrow, Annie. We'll precipitate a crisis tomorrow. Together. That's a promise."

Annie wished fervently that Matt would go back to being a domineering, high-handed, infuriating cowboy. She could fight him then. She was utterly defenseless against his gentle persuasion. But as she thought of the night ahead, the inevitable lovemaking and the further deepening of her feelings for him, she panicked again and shook herself free of his grasp. "Trust me for once, Mr. Harper," she said, heading determinedly for the door. "I'm a professional. I won't do anything stupid, and *that's* a promise."

Matt watched her leave, knowing there was no point in continuing to argue with her. All he could do was hope that Annie's fear of loving him wouldn't cloud her judgment.

But his banker and his accountant, he decided, were in for the fastest meeting of their lives.

At four o'clock, Elizabeth Reynolds was sitting in a chair opposite Annie's desk, her skin ashen, her eyes filled with tears. "He destroyed my life and then turned up to offer me a job, as if he were doing me some kind of favor," she said bitterly.

Annie suppressed her edginess and impatience. Matt's meeting could end any moment. She'd planned to have Elizabeth talking much sooner, but there'd been a detail to take care of first in the interest of safety. And the woman had been stubborn. She hadn't caved in until Annie had mentioned calling the police to suggest they get a search warrant for Elizabeth's apartment to check out her typewriter. "What did your husband tell you, Elizabeth?" she asked gently.

"The whole thing," Elizabeth snapped. "The pie-in-the-sky investment syndicate Matt talked Joe into."

So that was the story Joe had given his wife, Annie mused. He hadn't been very original.

"A Harper could afford to lose twenty thousand dollars on useless mining stocks," Elizabeth muttered. "But we couldn't. We had to mortgage our home and fork over the money to Matt Harper. I saw the check. Joe never recovered from the blow, and neither did our marriage."

"Joe was fond of the track, wasn't he?" Annie said very quietly.

Elizabeth leapt to her feet. "That's a lie!"

"And he walked out on you after losing everything to loan sharks," Annie added calmly. "He left you to fend for yourself, and the only person who was there for you was Matt Harper, riding in like a knight in shining armor. Only Matt didn't rescue you. He just gave you a chance to rescue yourself. You mistook his kindness for a romantic interest in you. You fantasized about getting even with Joe by landing Matt Harper. It was understandable, Elizabeth. All the things you went through could do strange things to anybody. But Matt didn't cooperate. He kept going out with other women."

"What does he see in *you*?" Elizabeth suddenly demanded. She wiped her eyes with the back of her hand, then opened her purse as if to get out a tissue.

Annie knew what was coming. She stood up and walked around her desk. "Elizabeth, think before you make any rash moves," she warned the woman. "So far all you've done is write some nasty letters. Don't go too far."

Elizabeth yanked out a gun and shakily aimed it at Annie. "Why not? What's the difference?"

"The difference is that you can destroy yourself or you can quit now and start putting yourself back together."

"All I'm interested in is destroying Matt Harper. And I've seen the way he looks at you. You're the key. I'll hurt him a lot worse by—"

Annie's door opened. She swore silently. Matt *would* have to end his meeting early!

"Okay, Annie," he said cheerfully. "I'm through for the day. What do you say we skip out—" He froze. "Annie," he whispered. "No. Dear God, no." His mind raced through a kaleidoscope of decisions. His impulse was to grab for Elizabeth's wrist, but he was too far from the woman; she could pull the trigger, and his Annie was at point-blank range. Yet to stand and wait helplessly, hoping Elizabeth would lose her nerve? He wasn't sure he could, and he cursed himself. Why had he let Annie out of his sight? Why hadn't he stood firm against her defiant bravado?

"Here's your chance, Elizabeth," Annie said

calmly, willing Matt to stay right where he was. "But you won't hurt me. You don't believe the lies Joe told you."

Elizabeth stared at her. "What makes you so sure?"

Annie just shook her head sadly. "You're in a lot of pain, Elizabeth, but you're a good person . . . not a violent person." She looked at the gun and held out her hand. "Wouldn't you like me to take care of that thing before it does some damage?"

Matt held his breath. If Annie lived through this moment, he promised himself, *he* was going to kill her. Several times over. The seconds passed with excruciating slowness. He debated again whether he could make it to the gun in time.

Then Elizabeth dropped the weapon to the carpet and buried her face in her hands. "I can't," she sobbed. "I just can't do it."

To Matt's admiration and amazement, Annie walked over and put her arms around the woman. "Of course you can't, Elizabeth. I never believed you could."

Matt wished he could say the same.

"Thrash is a good word," Matt muttered as he shut his apartment door after a long day and evening with the police, the lawyer he'd called in to help Elizabeth, and the psychiatrist he'd hired to work with her. "I remember hearing my dad tell Victoria he ought to thrash her. That's what I'll do to you. I'll thrash you."

"Try it," Annie said good-naturedly. She thought Matt was wonderful for the way he'd handled the situation with Elizabeth. There was no rancor toward the woman, only a genuine desire to do what he thought was the correct yet compassionate thing. Walking away from him was going to be more heart-wrenching than she'd ever thought.

"You're so tough," Matt said, resting his hands on Annie's shoulders. "I hope you're tough enough to handle being a young widow, because you knocked twenty years off my life today with that stunt."

"Mr. Harper, do you think I have Swiss cheese for brains? I'm a professional! I told you right from the start that I don't belong to the Mickey Spillane school of guns and gore. The minute I got a match on those typefaces and saw Elizabeth madly typing something into her computer that didn't look much like columns of figures, I knew she was cracking up. I decided what I was going to do, and I did it, though it took a little longer than I'd planned. Otherwise you'd never have walked in on—" She stopped suddenly and cocked her head to one side as something Matt had said belatedly registered. She wondered if she'd heard right.

"How did you get hold of that gun to empty it?" Matt demanded. "How did you know there *was* a gun?"

Annie was too distracted to say anything for a moment. Had Matt really said the word *widow*? Impossible. She gave herself a mental shake and answered his question. "I took a sealed envelope for Elizabeth's boss to the security desk downstairs and asked the guard to call Elizabeth in five minutes to pick it up. While she was gone I tiptoed over and grabbed her purse, saw the letter she'd just written and stuffed into the bag, found the gun, dumped out the bullets, replaced everything, then tiptoed back to my office and got ready to call her in. A regular Pink Panther operation."

"Why the big dramatic scene with Elizabeth? Why didn't you just report what you'd found?"

"Because I wanted a confession, of course. Nothing left to chance, slippery lawyers, or dozy judges. I also wanted Elizabeth to face herself and realize she wasn't capable of carrying out her crazy threats." Annie stiffened her backbone and told herself that a clean break would be easier in the long run. "So all's well that ends well, as old Willie the Bard says. Case closed. I'm off the job, outta here. I'll just pick up my belongings—"

"So will I," Matt said, sweeping Annie into his arms.

"Your belongings?" she said in a strangled voice.

"That's right, sweetheart. My belongings."

"Where do you get off making a suggestion like that?" Annie asked shakily.

"You'll find out," Matt shot back. "There's a lot to be settled between the two of us."

Annie refused to twine her arms around his neck. Refused to let herself get excited. Refused to allow her blood to heat with desire and hope and an all-consuming love. "Don't you try to bully me," she warned with all the firmness she could muster.

"I won't try," he said. "I'll just go ahead and do it, the way I should have done this afternoon. I'm through falling for your hard-boiled act, so you can stick out that pretty chin all you like and bluster about how a little Boston blueblood won't take any guff from anybody. That scare you gave me today sealed your fate, baby. From now on you're going to listen to me, and listen hard."

From now on, Annie thought. And *had* he said the word widow? She was dying to ask. But if he hadn't, her question would embarrass her beyond redemption. "Forget the John Wayne dialogue," she said instead. "And put me down."

"Don't give orders, Annie. Ask nicely."

"*You* don't seem to mind giving orders," she countered. Her heart began racing as she realized that Matt was carrying her toward his bedroom. If he took her there, she was lost. She loved the things that happened in that room. If she ended up there again, she would never want to leave. Love-'Em-and-Leave-'Em Harper would have to drag her out, kicking and screaming, when he was ready to move on. And *that* scene would be truly humiliating. "Will you stop making like a saddle tramp who's still galloping around in the nineteenth century when men supposedly were men and women supposedly liked them that way?"

"No," Matt answered, pushing open the bedroom door with his foot.

She realized she was going to have to play by his rules. "All right. Let me ask nicely. Would you please put me down?"

Matt smiled. "That's better, baby. And since you say it that way, of course I'll put you down." He proceeded to lower her to the bed and stretch out over her, gently pinning her hands to the mattress on either side of her head.

"I . . . I think you misinterpreted my meaning," Annie said raggedly as a hot, helpless desire instantly surged through her.

"And I think I'm interpreting your meaning a

whole lot better than you are," he murmured, then added gravely, "Annie, now that I've stopped playing games, why have you started?"

She stared up at him. "What do you mean?"

He touched his lips to hers, then raised his head and smiled down at her. "If you're going to be a Texan, you have to learn to be a straight shooter."

"I have no intention of being a Texan," she protested, deliberately begging the issue. "I'm going back East where I belong."

"You belong here," Matt informed her in a tone that brooked no argument. "And you know it. But let's get back to the point. When are you going to drop this act and be honest with me?"

"Honest? Honest about what?"

He shook his head in mock frustration. "Okay, maybe you need a little coaching. Maybe somebody here has to set the example. So I'll do it. Here's the kind of honesty I'm talking about: I love you, Annie Brentwood."

Annie caught her breath and her eyes instantly filled with tears again. "That's impossible!"

Matt had anticipated a number of possible responses to the confession of love he'd been wanting to make for days. *That's impossible* wasn't one of them. "Why is it impossible?" he asked, touching his lips to her forehead, then her brows and temples and cheeks.

"Because you . . . because I . . . I . . . well, we . . ." she gave up. She couldn't think.

"I see," Matt said patiently. "Well, how can I argue with someone who's being so articulate? But the fact remains, I do love you, Annie. I love you. I'm not kidding around here. I'm talking commitment, in capital letters." He took a deep breath and let it out slowly, his eyes locked on hers. "And now, Annie, it's your turn."

She stared up at him, trying to hold back her tears. She was too stunned to speak. Too moved to shatter the incredible moment with a sound. Too frightened to let herself believe it was real.

"C'mon, sweetheart. It's easier than you think," Matt coaxed. "I'll get your started. Repeat after me: I . . ."

Annie's lips curved in a tiny smile. "I," she echoed softly.

"Love," Matt said, his eyes darkening as he gazed down at her.

"Lo . . ." Annie stopped, then let the tears flow. "Oh Matt, I love you. I love you so much, dammit."

He lowered his mouth to hers. "That's the way, baby," he whispered. "I knew you could be romantic if you tried."

Hours later, as Annie nestled against Matt's broad chest, still not sure where things were going from this point, she heard her unspoken question being answered.

"We can announce our engagement at the barbecue," Matt suddenly said.

Annie's heart skipped several beats, and she closed her eyes to absorb the moment of pure joy. Then she propped herself up on one elbow. "Interesting," she said. "Except there's one little problem: We're not engaged."

Matt gave her a surprised look. "Sure we are. You know as well as I do that what we've committed ourselves to is marriage. By the way, I'm really

looking forward to having you meet the rest of
the clan. You're going to love them."

"Is that an order?" Annie asked, though she
was convinced she would adore every last Harper
in Texas just for having the same name as Matt.

"It's a prediction," he answered with a grin.
"And there's no question that they'll be crazy
about you."

Annie suddenly grew serious. "Matt, don't tease
me this way. You haven't proposed. And even if
you did, I'm not sure I'd believe it. I don't want
to buy into all these hearts and flowers only to be
stuck with a wilted bouquet when you decide to
leave. We hardly know each other. You can't mean
what you're saying about marriage."

"You don't think I mean it? Try me, baby," Matt
said, his voice thick with emotion. He wished he
hadn't spent so much energy teaching Annie not
to trust him. It was going to take a lot of effort
and patience and love to reverse the effects of his
stupid campaign, not to mention the idiotic wom-
anizing reputation he'd been foolish enough to
foster, just for the sake of avoiding romantic
entanglements. Even his mother had bought it.
"Annie, stand me up in front of a preacher and
see what happens," he added softly. "Did you hear
me earlier? I love you. I want to marry you. I'll
never leave you. How could I? You're my other
half, and I'm yours, and we've both felt that con-
nection from the first moment we met. I dream
of spending the rest of my days with you—and
only you. I keep seeing little Annies and little Mat-
thews running around the ranch playing cowboys
and gumshoes. What do I have to do to make you
trust me? Name it and I'll do it as penance. And
by the way, we *have* known each other long

enough. How many people who date for months spend as much time together as we have in the past couple of weeks? But if it makes you happy, I'll agree to a long engagement. We could put off the wedding until, say, a week from next Friday."

Annie tried to suppress the hope that was overcoming her common sense. "We'd be a terrible match," she said feebly.

Matt reached for her and hauled her back into his arms. "We'd be perfect. We're a great match. We're both stubborn."

"Exactly," she said, beginning to tremble with a sudden, overwhelming wave of emotion. "You'd pull some stunt to make me mad, we'd have a fight, and neither of us would back down. Fifty years later we'd still be going at it."

"At least we'd be together," he said with a grin as he crooked his index finger under Annie's chin and made her look up at him. Aware that this woman had a power over him such as he'd never dreamed possible, he figured he'd better at least pay lip service to protecting his image as a rough, tough, unyielding cowboy. "But you're wrong, Annie. We won't fight. I'm a Texan, remember? I know how to keep a soft-hearted little Easterner in line."

"Oh really?" Annie said, gathering strength for a small rebellion. "And just how—?"

A moment later, dizzy from a kiss that answered all her questions, Annie was still trying to resist, but with severely weakened defenses. "Victoria won't agree to this marriage," she murmured, no longer sure why she was grasping at straws. "She hired me as a bodyguard, not a prospective daughter-in-law."

Matt laughed and showered kisses over Annie's

face and throat. "Wrong, honey. I told Victoria yesterday that I wanted to marry you, and she informed me it was damn well time I realized it. Of course, we both insist you're to take no more bodyguarding assignments. I'll even have it written into our marriage vows."

"I wouldn't want to take any more jobs like this one," Annie retorted shakily as Matt's caresses vanquished the last bit of fight left in her. "I didn't want *this* one. But don't you see how unsuitable I am for you? You need a proper lady in your life, not a Miss Effie dropout."

"I need a Lost Cause," he countered. "I need you."

Annie thought of one more obstacle. "You've yet to meet the snobbish Brentwoods."

Matt smiled tenderly at her as he moved his hand over her body with easy, knowing possessiveness. "I give you my solemn oath that I'll charm them right out of their ancestral trees."

"You probably will," Annie murmured, sighing with pleasure. "If I marry you, I'll have spoiled my rebel image forever. My staid New England family will probably approve of me for the first time in my misbegotten life."

"I wouldn't worry about it too much, baby," Matt said with a wicked gleam in his blue-green eyes. "Between the two of us, we'll come up with something that'll get you banned in Boston all over again."

The last shreds of Annie's resistance suddenly dissolved. "Mr. Harper," she whispered as she reached up to cradle his face between her palms, "perhaps you should show me some more about how a Texan keeps his wife in line. I think I'm going to need a lot of instruction on that score."

"Aren't you forgetting one little detail?" he asked with loving determination. "Isn't there a certain word you want to say to me?"

Annie smiled. "Aren't you forgetting what precedes that certain word?"

Moving over Annie and sliding his arms under her to lift her to him, Matt chuckled. The last word, he suspected, would always be his wife's. And he didn't mind a bit. "Annie Brentwood, will you marry me?" he asked, his lips against her ear.

Annie sifted her fingers through his silky, tousled hair. "Of course I will, silly," she murmured. "Whatever made you think I wouldn't?"

THE EDITOR'S CORNER

Each month we have LOVESWEPTs that dazzle . . . that warm the heart or bring laughter and the occasional tear—all of them sensual and full of love, of course. Seldom, however, are all six books literally sizzling with so much fiery passion and tumultuous romance as next month's.

First, a love story sure to blaze in your memory is remarkable Billie Green's **STARBRIGHT**, LOVESWEPT #456. Imagine a powerful man with midnight-blue eyes and a former model who has as much heart and soul as she does beauty. He is brilliant lawyer Garrick Fane, a man with a secret. She is Elise Adler Bright, vulnerable and feisty, who believes Garrick has betrayed her. When a terrifying accident hurls them together, they have one last chance to explore their fierce physical love . . . and the desperate problems each has tried to hide. As time runs out for them, they must recapture the true love they'd once believed was theirs—or lose it forever. Fireworks sparked with humor. A sizzler, indeed.

Prepare to soar when you read LOVESWEPT #457, **PASSION'S FLIGHT,** by talented Terry Lawrence. Sensual, sensual, sensual is this story of a legendary dancer and notorious seducer known throughout the world as "Stash." He finds the woman he can love faithfully for a lifetime in Mariah Heath. Mariah is also a dancer and one Stash admires tremendously for her grace and fierce emotionality. But he is haunted by a past that closes him to enduring love—and Mariah must struggle to break through her own vulnerabilities to teach her incredible over that forever can be theirs. This is a romance that's as unforgettable as it is delectable.

As steamy as the bayou, as exciting as Bourbon Street in New Orleans, **THE RESTLESS HEART**, LOVESWEPT #458, by gifted Tami Hoag, is sure to win your heart. Tami has really given us a gift in the hero she's created for this romance. What a wickedly handsome, mischievous, and sexy Cajun Remy Doucet is! And how he woos heroine Danielle Hamilton. From diapering babies to kissing a lady senseless, Remy is masterful. But a lie and a shadow stand between him and Danielle . . . and only when a dangerous misunderstanding parts them can they find truth and the love they deserve. Reading not to be missed!

Guaranteed to start a real conflagration in your imagination is extraordinary Sandra Chastain's **FIREBRAND**, LOVESWEPT #459. Cade McCall wasn't the kind of man to answer an ad as mysterious as Rusty Wilder's—but he'd never needed a job so badly. When he met the green-eyed rancher whose wild red hair echoed her spirit, he fell hard. Rusty found Cade too handsome, too irresistible to become the partner she needed. Consumed by the flames of desire they generated, only searing romance could follow . . . but each feared their love might turn to ashes if he or she couldn't tame the other. Silk and denim . . . fire and ice. A LOVESWEPT that couldn't have been better titled—**FIREBRAND**.

Delightful Janet Evanovich outdoes herself with **THE ROCKY ROAD TO ROMANCE**, LOVESWEPT #460, which sparkles with fiery fun. In the midst of a wild and woolly romantic chase between Steve Crow and Daisy Adams, you should be prepared to meet an old and fascinating friend—that quirky Elsie Hawkins. This is Elsie's fourth appearance in Janet's LOVESWEPTS. All of us have come to look forward to where she'll turn up next . . . and just how she'll affect the outcome of a stalled romance. Elsie won't disappoint you as she works her wondrous ways on the smoldering romance of Steve and Daisy. A real winner!

Absolutely breathtaking! A daring love story not to be missed! Those were just a couple of the remarks heard in the office from those who read **TABOO,** LOVESWEPT #461, by Olivia Rupprecht. Cammie Walker had been adopted by Grant Kennedy's family when her family died in a car crash. She grew up with great brotherly love for Grant. Then, one night when Cammie came home to visit, she saw Grant as she'd never seen him before. Her desire for him was overwhelming . . . unbearably so. And Grant soon confessed he'd been passionately in love with her for years. But Cammie was terrified of their love . . . and terrified of how it might affect her adopted parents. **TABOO** is one of the most emotionally touching and stunningly sensual romances of the year.

And do make sure you look for the three books next month in Bantam's fabulous imprint, FANFARE . . . the very best in women's popular fiction. It's a spectacular FANFARE month with **SCANDAL** by Amanda Quick, **STAR-CROSSED LOVERS** by Kay Hooper, and **HEAVEN SENT** by newcomer Pamela Morsi.

Enjoy!

Sincerely,

Carolyn Nichols

Carolyn Nichols,
Publisher,
LOVESWEPT
Bantam Books
666 Fifth Avenue
New York, NY 10103

THE LATEST IN BOOKS
AND AUDIO CASSETTES

Paperbacks

☐	28671	**NOBODY'S FAULT** Nancy Holmes	$5.95
☐	28412	**A SEASON OF SWANS** Celeste De Blasis	$5.95
☐	28354	**SEDUCTION** Amanda Quick	$4.50
☐	28594	**SURRENDER** Amanda Quick	$4.50
☐	28435	**WORLD OF DIFFERENCE** Leonia Blair	$5.95
☐	28416	**RIGHTFULLY MINE** Doris Mortman	$5.95
☐	27032	**FIRST BORN** Doris Mortman	$4.95
☐	27283	**BRAZEN VIRTUE** Nora Roberts	$4.50
☐	27891	**PEOPLE LIKE US** Dominick Dunne	$4.95
☐	27260	**WILD SWAN** Celeste De Blasis	$5.95
☐	25692	**SWAN'S CHANCE** Celeste De Blasis	$5.95
☐	27790	**A WOMAN OF SUBSTANCE** Barbara Taylor Bradford	$5.95

Audio

☐	**SEPTEMBER** by Rosamunde Pilcher Performance by Lynn Redgrave 180 Mins. Double Cassette 45241-X	$15.95
☐	**THE SHELL SEEKERS** by Rosamunde Pilcher Performance by Lynn Redgrave 180 Mins. Double Cassette 48183-9	$14.95
☐	**COLD SASSY TREE** by Olive Ann Burns Performance by Richard Thomas 180 Mins. Double Cassette 45166-9	$14.95
☐	**NOBODY'S FAULT** by Nancy Holmes Performance by Geraldine James 180 Mins. Double Cassette 45250-9	$14.95

60 Minutes to a Better, More Beautiful You!

Now it's easier than ever to awaken your sensuality, stay slim forever—even make yourself irresistible. With Bantam's bestselling subliminal audio tapes, you're only 60 minutes away from a better, more beautiful you!